TO CATCH AN ELF

PENNSYLVANIA FIGHTER PILOT

DEBRA PARMLEY

This book is dedicated to my readers, who have waited a very long time for the completion of this story. I appreciate every single one of you, and I hope you enjoy reading To Catch an Elf.

CHAPTER 1

MEETING THE ELF ...

Zeke Kingsley and Beverly Westwood were holding hands in Upstate New York, strolling past quaint little shops that bored him to death, when he spotted an antique Christmas elf sitting behind a store window, staring out at him.

The elf wore red-and-white striped pants with a green vest covered with stars, along with a red belt with a gold buckle. A red-and-white striped hat with tiny bells sat atop her long blonde hair in braids. Her long legs and arms were bendable for posing. Pointed green shoes with bells finished her outfit.

She was unique, unlike any Christmas elf that Zeke had ever seen.

People all over the country would post pictures of their elves on the Biggest Busy Elf Contest website.

All to try to win a five-thousand-dollar prize. Beverly had decided to enter the contest and she wanted to win.

That elf is perfect.

He almost laughed out loud as he stopped suddenly.

When Zeke didn't step forward with her, but stopped

and tugged her back toward him, Beverly turned with a frown.

"I've found you the perfect elf, for your elf contest," he said. Then he pointed to it.

Her frown deepened as she looked at the doll.

"It's unique," he said. "No one else will have one like it. Let's go in."

"No." Beverly adamantly shook her head. "Antique shops are dreadful, stinky stores full of old things that smell." She crinkled her perfect nose, and adjusted her fur coat around her shoulders, as if she were suddenly chilled.

Which made no sense, as it was a warm fall evening and would not begin to cool off for another hour.

He watched her, thinking.

Had to be her reaction to the store, or to the elf. Interesting.

His high-society girlfriend was suddenly showing cracks in her normal façade for the first time since he'd known her.

Everyone had a face they presented to the world, and one they used in the dark, when no one else was around. That had been his early discovery as a child, watching grownups, and his adult life in college and beyond hadn't shown him anything different.

I wonder what caused her extreme dislike of antique shops and the old things they display. She likely wouldn't enjoy historical museums either.

"Never mind," he said. "If you're cold, we can stop for a cappuccino instead."

"That sounds much better," Beverly said, her usual mask back in place.

With her perfect nose, porcelain skin, cool blue eyes, and platinum blonde hair, she could have stepped out of a fashion magazine.

And she knew it.

That, and her family money, gave her a haughty air at times.

Beverly also loved to show off her double D breasts that her family's old money had bought her. They always caught men's attention, and she loved the attention.

She flashed him a smile, one that would have had most men catering to her every whim.

It never worked on him.

The first time she'd tried it, he'd simply stood there watching her, for what most would have considered a very long time, before giving her a wink, to let her know he was onto her and unmoved by her charms.

Then he had walked away.

That made him as attractive as hell to her, as he knew it would.

He knew a thing or two about inheriting money and had kept his inheritance quiet, refusing to let anyone know how much he had, but implying that he had "enough." So, he could easily behave as if he did not care about her family money, or their influence.

Though, in truth, he believed that having more was always better. The more you had, the more you could do things that you otherwise couldn't.

He also had a knack for watching people, and learning things about them that they might not even have known themselves.

She saw him as strong in mind and character.

Beverly was right.

Never would he let another woman control him or emasculate him. He'd learned strength, growing up with a mother who controlled everything. Growing up without a father, he'd had no other choice as a child.

Just as his mother had shown one face to the world, and another to him at home, he too learned to present a mask.

The difference was, he never let his slip and never lost his temper. He was always in control of himself.

Beverly knew nothing of his past.

He'd told her that both of his parents were dead, and she'd dropped the subject at once, not wanting to hear of unpleasant things.

She tried to avoid hearing unpleasant things.

It did bring a degree of sympathy into her eyes after that, and if the subject came up, she would steer people away from it, as if she was doing him a kindness.

He really didn't care about that. He found watching her amusing.

She had no clue how much he watched her. Watching women was something he enjoyed.

They went on to have cappuccinos, and then to finish her early Christmas shopping.

October seemed early to him, but people did shop that early. He was more of a shop the night before kind of man and would pick from whatever was left in the stores to choose from.

To him, Christmas was no big deal. Other people didn't celebrate Christmas the way he would have.

Santa rarely brought him something he wanted.

This Christmas would be different.

LATER, when Zeke was back at work in Manhattan, he called the antique shop and described the elf.

"Do you still have the elf?" he asked.

"Yes, we still have it," the woman answered.

"Excellent," he said. "I'll purchase the elf, if you can send it out to be cleaned and to be filled with new stuffing."

"But that would decrease the value of the antique," the shop owner protested.

"True, but then I can gift it to my fiancée, who has terrible allergies. This is a Christmas gift, and I don't want it to make her sick. She will love the gift, but not if it has old stuffing. It must be hypoallergenic stuffing for her, all the way."

"Oh, I see," the woman said, though she was still clearly distressed at the idea of devaluing the antique.

He could tell by her tone, and by the fact that she had yet to agree to it.

"The elf is old and comes with a history," she said. "Her name is Tananna. The girl who owned her died and her mother took the doll and packed it away in a trunk, where it stayed until everything in the house was sold in an estate sale many years later. We've tried to find others like her, but there seem to be none. She is unique and should be preserved."

"I'm not going to change what she looks like. Just her stuffing. Can it be done? I will pay extra," he said.

Throwing more money at something often brought the result you wanted.

"Yes, it can be done," she said with a sigh, giving in. "I know people who restore dolls."

Zeke gave her his credit card number, and the purchase was made.

He would surprise Beverly with the elf, just before December and the start of the online elf contest.

They'd be spending the Christmas holiday in Miami, Florida.

Beverly would need a dog-sitter, and house-sitter for her

house in the Large Bass Lake subdivision in the Pocono Mountains.

A house she never went to unless she wanted to ski all weekend. Which she only did once a year now that the newness had worn off. Once the newness wore off anything, she was done with it.

He knew all about newness wearing off. But he had the perfect house-sitter for her, one who house sat for his cousin not long ago.

A blonde named Marcie, with curves and a sweet smile, who also loved dogs.

She was perfect.

AFTER THE ELF ARRIVED, he looked the doll over. You could see the recent stitching, where they'd cut the back of the fabric of the doll and then stitched it back together There was plenty of new stuffing.

Good.

Taking scissors, he ripped open the stitching, careful not to cut anything that would leave a mark.

Then he pulled out just enough stuffing and inserted a camera inside. Threading the thin part, that would sit behind the eye of the doll up into her face, behind the eye, he fiddled with it until everything was in place. Then made sure the stuffing hid everything, so you could not feel the equipment.

After that, he restitched the doll. It took a while, because no one had taught him how to sew, but eventually he got it done.

Finished, he looked the doll over.

No one will know.

He would give Beverly the doll tomorrow night.

BEVERLY STILL DIDN'T LIKE the elf much. Even though the doll now smelled fresh and new and had been cleaned.

"What is this?" She leaned back against his leather couch, away from the doll. "Why would you buy this old thing for me?"

"I bought her for you, so you can win," he spoke as if it should be obvious. "This elf is unique, no one else will have one like it. The owner of the shop tried to locate another one like it and had no luck, so this must be the only one in existence. The other contestants will be buying new elves off the shelves. I know how you can't stand to see any woman wearing the same dress as you, so I don't believe you'd want your elf to look like everyone else's. Look, I even had her cleaned and re-stuffed for you, so there's no bad smell."

His tone implied that he'd gone to a lot of trouble for her.

She appeared confused.

"Her insides are all new?" she asked, though he'd just told her that they were.

Patient, he nodded.

"Well," she hesitated, picking the doll up and giving it a quick sniff, to double-check.

He knew it didn't smell bad.

"Thank you," she finally said. "I do want to win the contest."

She sat the doll back down on the coffee table and stared at it for a long time.

Finally, she spoke. "It's looking at me."

"Most dolls do," he said. "And you've been staring at it for a while. Don't make yourself paranoid over a silly doll."

"Well, I'm not taking this elf to Miami with us," she said. "I don't want to have to look at her, or have her looking at me, every time we come back to our room."

"You don't have to take the elf to Miami," he said. "Let the house-sitter take the pictures for the contest and send them to you. It's not like she'll have anything else to do, besides walking the dog once a day."

Ginger, Beverly's little King Charles Spaniel, was easy to take care of, this was true. She just needed to be fed, watered, and walked. Which was all Beverly did with her. The rest of the time Ginger was at doggie daycare. But they didn't board dogs overnight.

"That's a great idea," Beverly said. "Didn't you say you knew someone?"

"Yes," he said. "My cousin hired a house-sitter a few months ago, and she was good. I'll call him for her contact number and take care of it. And, if you don't want to take the elf home with you tonight, she can stay here until you hand her off to the sitter."

He didn't tell her the house-sitter's name was Marcie Hayes, or that he'd had Marcie's number for months. He'd even had Marcie investigated. He knew a lot about Marcie Hayes that his girlfriend didn't need to know.

She didn't need to know a lot of things. Luckily, she was too busy being pretty to be more inquisitive.

Beverly gave him a beautiful smile, and then leaned forward and kissed him.

His smile after that kiss was deep.

Not merely because of the kiss.

He was visualizing Marcie with her soft curves, big blue

eyes, and long blonde hair. She was pretty enough to be a doll herself. Pretty enough to be in pictures with the elf.

The elf would keep her company all through December, as she took pictures with it, for the elf contest.

And he would be watching.

It was the perfect plan.

~

Day one: Take a picture of you meeting the elf ...

THE STRANGEST REQUEST Marcie Hayes had received since she'd started her 'Home Sweet Home Sitting' house-sitting business, five years ago, sat on the kitchen table staring at her.

She stared back.

Ginger, the little dog she would be dog-sitting, had been barking since she'd walked in the front door, but she was supposed to read this note first, even before letting the dog out.

An antique Christmas elf sat on the table beside the note.

To be honest, Marcie found the Christmas elf more than a little creepy, with its weird eyes, and she thought, not for the first time since walking into the room, that its eyes were following her.

But doll eyes didn't follow people because dolls weren't alive. So, she brushed her initial thoughts aside.

Christmas elves of the stuffed variety, which had become popular, were supposed to be Santa's helpers, reporting back to Santa on whether a child had been good or not.

Though this antique elf didn't look the same as those

elves and did not look like an elf anyone should ever give a child, it was still a Christmas elf.

People all over the country would post pictures of their elves on the Biggest Busy Elf Contest website.

All to try to win the five-thousand-dollar prize. And Beverly wanted to win.

Marcie glanced down again at the instructions Beverly Westwood had left for her on the table in front of the elf. Picking up the paper she reread the part about the elf.

Meet Tananna, my Christmas elf. Isn't she wonderful? I'll bet no one has an elf just like her. She's an antique from one of those Slav countries. Czechoslovakia, or Poland, or Croatia, or something.

Marcie shook her head and thought: *She's covering such a wide range of Slav countries; she has no idea where it's from.* Marcie went back to reading the note.

I want to win the Biggest Busy Elf Contest, so this is very important. I want you to take a picture of my elf every day and text it to me. The grand prize this year is five thousand dollars! The pictures you take must be good. No blurry or off-centered ones.

I want one taken in each room of the house (so make sure it stays clean) doing Christmas stuff. I will tell you exactly what to do, so it will be easy.

We can do this! We can win! Here is the schedule:

Day one: Take a pic of you meeting the elf in the kitchen.

Day two: The elf watching you make breakfast. Make it a big breakfast. Bacon, fried eggs, toast, and hash-browns. Remember, everyone will see the picture! Position her so she is watching the pans on the stove while you cook, but not close enough that the elf might catch fire. Remember, she is old and is a valuable antique.

Marcie had to put the note back down on the table, and

step away as her emotions charged up. "She's telling me what to eat!" She voiced her opinion to the empty kitchen.

The little King Charles Spaniel started barking even more.

She needed to hurry through this note and let the dog out.

"I never eat a big breakfast!"

More barking answered her.

Usually, she just had a simple bowl of cereal or oatmeal.

"Now I must cook a big, greasy breakfast?" she muttered to herself. "I don't think so."

She paced and thought.

Beverly must be a control freak.

Only a control freak would tell someone else what to do, even down to what they had to eat. Only a control freak would attempt to control what was going on when they weren't around.

"I am not letting someone else tell me what to eat or drink. It's my body. I alone have the say in what goes into it."

Barking, barking, barking answered her.

She went back to the table and read the rest of the note.

Day three: Take a picture of the elf helping you put up the Christmas tree. The tree and decorations are all in the basement, clearly marked with which ones to use this year.

"Good gravy," Marcie said. "This woman is something else." She read faster.

Day four: Watch a Christmas DVD with the elf, in the living room. Watch the Rudolph movie for this picture. Make popcorn and use the Santa bowl.

Day five: Take a picture of the elf on the desk with the phone, reporting to Santa.

Day six: Take a picture of the elf on the bookshelf in the downstairs office/study picking out a Christmas story to read.

Day seven: Take a picture of the elf having hot cocoa. Then show her climbing up the tree because she's had too much sugar. Make sure no bulbs get broken. That is taking the naughty elf too far.

"I know who's taking things too far," Marcie muttered, ignoring the barking dog, which was starting to upset her, as usually she did not ignore people's dogs. She hurried to get through reading the message to the end.

Day eight: Take a picture of you and the elf, in the kitchen, baking Christmas cookies. The sugar cut-out kind. I want the kind you make from scratch, not the slice-and-bake ones, and no store-bought ready-made! There needs to be flour on the table, and the elf with the rolling pin.

"She doesn't even know if I can bake or cook. Nothing about food, or diet, or cooking was mentioned to me when I took this job." Marcie shook her head. "Unreal." She continued to read.

Day nine: Naughty elf takes a bite out of one of the cookies. Take a picture of the elf, and the rest of the cookie.

Day ten: Take a picture of the elf writing a letter to Santa.

"I know what I'd like to write to Santa about," Marcie said.

Day eleven: Take a picture of the elf upstairs in bed with you, reading a bedtime Christmas story. Be sure to wear cute pajamas.

"Now she's telling me what to wear," Marcie muttered. "I never agreed to be in pictures posted online, in bed, wearing cute pajamas. I don't even wear pajamas."

The white silk nightie she wore, which was her soft comfort sleep item and traveled with her, was not something she was willing to wear in pictures spread over the internet. Too much of her showed through it. But it was the softest, silkiest thing she had ever owned and sleeping in it was a way of pampering herself, something she needed when staying in other people's bedrooms.

"We're going to have to talk about this," Marcie said. "First, she isn't paying me enough to do all this, and second, I'm not wearing what she says, or eating what she says."

Marcie noted there was no offer to pay for all the food she was supposed to cook, or to pay for pajamas to appear in. Not that she was doing any of that stuff anyway. But, if she were inclined, it would not be coming out of her pay.

She went back to reading the list.

Day twelve: Take a bubble bath with the elf and set her on the shelf at the end of the tub where she won't really get wet. Just put some bubbles on her.

In disgust, Marcie stopped reading the list.

"So, I'm dog-sitting, house-sitting, and baby-sitting an elf doll, while the owner tells me what to eat and wear, and she wants me to take a bubble bath ... with an elf."

She hook her head. "This is crazy. And *none* of this was part of our original agreement. She owns the house and its contents and the dog. She does not own me. I provide a service she has paid for, which is not the same thing at all."

She skimmed down to the bottom of the elf pictures list, from day twelve on, and then read the final entries.

Day twenty-three: The day before Christmas Eve, the contest is over.

Day twenty-four: Christmas Eve, be ready to take a picture of the elf with the winning email when we win!

I know we have an edge because my elf is a very special antique elf. She doesn't stink like other antiques because she's been cleaned and restored, and even has new stuffing. You won't see another elf like her on the internet, or anywhere else.

Not sure where Zeke found her, but she's the best gift ever.

I want you to think of her as your new best friend. She'll do everything with you this season, so you won't be alone, and you'll also have Ginger.

Ginger may bark at her, but she's just being silly.

Use your imagination and have lots of fun with the contest! The more pictures the better, that way I'll have plenty to choose from.

And you will receive a fifty-dollar bonus if we win!

No wonder Beverly wanted to try to cash in on the prize. But she wanted Marcie to do all the work. And she hadn't offered Marcie any portion of that good prize if they won.

Just a fifty-dollar bonus.

Fifty dollars wouldn't even cover all the groceries and other stuff she'd have to buy to meet all of Beverly's demands.

The only thing Beverly had to do was upload the pictures using her code into the form on the website. Her pictures would all be grouped together somehow by using that code.

Marcie would have to take the elf pictures and then send them to Beverly in Miami, where she was on holiday with her boyfriend, Zeke.

She'd gotten the job, because of Zeke, though she barely remembered meeting him, before she got in her car to leave a house-sitting job for his cousin.

The cousins had arrived at the homeowner's house together, after a trip.

She may not have remembered him, but he had remembered her.

Zeke had suggested her to his girlfriend, Beverly, when she'd needed a house-sitter and a dog-sitter.

Now here Marcie was, house-sitting a house in the Large Bass Lake subdivision in the Poconos, in December, and dog-sitting a King Charles Spaniel named Ginger, along with a creepy elf named Tananna.

Well, best to get on with it.

She moved the irritating note out of the way, pulled out her cell phone and selfie stick to take a picture and frowned. Then she stood next to the elf, forced a smile, and took the first photo on the list.

She texted it to Beverly.

The things I do for my clients. Sigh. Is this going to raise my phone bill?

I'm only going to send her one picture a day. Take as many as I want? I don't want to take any. So, unless I get a pay increase, one will have to do.

Opening the refrigerator, on the way out of the kitchen, before going to let Ginger out, she found bottled water, condiments, and a tomato.

So, where's the food I'm supposed to cook for the big breakfast? Not in this refrigerator. That would mean a grocery bill, which she won't reimburse me for, and it would mean going to the grocery tonight for this breakfast to happen tomorrow morning.

She frowned and shook her head. *No, Beverly. Not happening.*

Marcie considered what she knew about the woman she was house sitting for.

Very little. Less than she usually knew about a client.

What's she really like?

Marcie had only spoken to Beverly once on the phone, after Zeke had set up the meeting.

The woman was certainly a control freak, but one of the nice things about house-sitting was the fact that the home-owner was away and not in your face, forcing you to have to deal with their micromanaging.

With a phone call, you could distance yourself a little,

put them on speakerphone, and move across the room to fold your laundry, or do whatever else needed doing.

Best way to deal with anyone going off on a rant was to get distance.

She took out a bottle of water, uncapped it, and took a swallow.

Now to meet Ginger.

The little dog had been barking since Marcie had let herself into the house with the key that had been under the mat on the front deck.

Ordinarily, she would have put meeting the dog first on her list.

She'd been told to go find the note first, to read it before letting Ginger out, and to put the key back under the mat, where the cleaning lady could find it.

Beverly was going to have the house "thoroughly cleaned," but she didn't say when, or leave any information about the cleaning lady.

Marcie always did her best to follow her client's directions, so she put the key back under the mat, but she didn't feel good about it. It didn't seem like the safest idea. But, without knowing how to get ahold of the cleaning lady to make other arrangements, she didn't have much choice.

Usually, she would put the client's house key on her key ring right away and never take it off until the job was done. Then she'd return it exactly where she got it. She'd never lost a key or been locked out. Not once.

Ginger was still barking and sounded wound up. Probably because a stranger was in her house. The little dog had only been left alone for an hour, as Marcie had made sure to arrive as close to the time Beverly and her boyfriend Zeke had left as possible.

If her flight hadn't been delayed by an hour, she'd have been there right after they'd left, as planned.

I'll let Ginger out, and I'll check to make sure all the windows and doors are locked from the outside.

Later, she would check from the inside.

These habits were for her safety and had developed from moving into strange houses in towns she'd never been in before.

You couldn't always count on everything being secure. Homeowners were often careless, particularly when their minds were on going out of town.

It was Marcie's job to keep an eye on the house, contents and any pets, and it was one she took seriously. There'd never been a theft on her watch, and she intended to keep it that way.

So far, the front door to the living room and the sliding glass doors in the kitchen were the only doors she'd gone in or out of, but that didn't mean the others were locked, or that the windows were locked. People often forgot.

Here in ski country, did it ever get warm enough to open the windows?

None of the windows looked like they even opened. This was her first time staying on a mountain in ski country in a chalet-style house.

Maybe here, on top of the mountain, it didn't get warm enough to open windows.

She'd entered through the front door, and pocketed the key, then moved through the living room and then down the three steps off to the right, ending up in the kitchen, where the instructions were on the table.

Ginger barked and barked.

Marcie felt bad about not going to the little dog right away, but she was following the homeowner's instructions.

It was important to read the instructions first. Sometimes there were directions as to the care of the pet.

It's best to learn what you can about the pet, before meeting them. That way you'd hopefully learn anything important and could ease any distress the pet might feel at meeting a stranger who had entered their house.

This time she'd been given little information about the dog.

Beverly was more interested in the elf than her own dog.

The note had barely mentioned Ginger. There were no instructions for her care. Marcie sighed and tried not to be judgmental.

Checking the sliding glass doors, she paused to look out at the snow-covered view. A blanket of white covered everything.

The view sure is pretty.

Leaving the note on the table, she headed for her first meeting with Ginger, leaving the kitchen, moving past a small bathroom, and into the next room at the back of the house.

Ginger barked again.

"Coming, Ginger," she called. "I hear you, and I've heard all about you."

Actually, she hadn't. Hadn't been told where the dog crate was, what Ginger's favorite toys or food were, or any tips to make dog-sitting any easier for either of them.

The only thing she'd been told over the phone was, "You're a dog-sitter. You know what to do."

Well, yes, I do know what to do, but still. Beverly gave more instructions on that weird elf than she did on her own dog. And that elf just sits there. It doesn't need anything.

Her dog, Ginger, on the other hand, is a living creature, with a personality, feelings, and needs. You'd think being away for an entire month, her owner would care more about her dog than a silly old elf and an online contest. Money prize or not.

How does Ginger do with strangers? Well, I'll soon find out.

Inside the crate, a brown-and-white King Charles Spaniel barked and wagged her tail furiously. She had the sweetest face, and her coat was shiny and untangled.

She's been groomed. At least she looks cared for, not neglected. It's time to let her out.

The closer Marcie got; the more excited Ginger became.

Marcie laughed as she reached into her coat pocket, to touch the doggie treats she had brought with her. "You lost your warning bark, Ginger. That's a 'pet me please' bark, if I ever heard one."

Ginger's tail wagged even more furiously.

The minute Marcie unlatched the door, Ginger rushed out and stood barking happily, wagging her tail.

"Well, you are just adorable," Marcie said. She loved seeing happy dogs and knowing that she made them happy.

Ginger responded with kisses and tail wags, which wagged her whole body, making Marcie laugh.

Dog-sitting could be so much fun.

"It's nice to meet you too, girl," Marcie said. "Do you need to go out?"

The little dog responded with more wiggles and tail and body wags in her excitement. The soft, cuddly dog had plenty of energy and plenty of welcome kisses for her new dog-sitter.

Holding off on a treat for now, Marcie reached for a nearby leash and clipped it to Ginger's collar.

Once Ginger was on her leash, they moved past the bathroom and into the kitchen, toward the sliding glass doors, which led to the front deck.

Ginger stopped in front of the kitchen table, refusing to

go farther, and began barking furiously at the elf, as ferocious as a King Charles Spaniel could be, her tail no longer wagging. Instead, she went from barking to growling at the elf.

Marcie wasn't thrilled with the elf either, but she wondered what it was about the elf that had made the dog so upset.

The previously sweet-faced, happy little dog now appeared as if she wanted to tear that elf apart. The sudden switch in behavior was a bit unnerving, and Marcie wasn't sure how to handle the situation.

CHAPTER 2

arcie decided to try talking to the dog, and if
that didn't work, there were always the
doggie treats in her pocket.

Ginger continued barking and growling at the elf.

"Well, my goodness," Marcie said. "You don't like that elf
much, do you?"

Ginger barked again, louder, as if in confirmation.

"I don't blame you," Marcie said. "I think she's creepy."

Ginger barked once, as if saying yes, and then Marcie
reached to unlock and open the sliding glass doors.

The little dog nearly bounced outside. She was either
excited or needed to go, though it was likely her owner had
let her out right before she left.

If Beverly had been self-centered enough to forget, then
Ginger might really need to go.

"Okay, girl," Marcie said. "You go do your business and
then we'll take a walk so you can get some exercise."

The walk would consist of one close circle around the
house to check on everything for security, another part of

Marcie's routine. Then she would explore through the trees around the back of the house with Ginger.

Marcie would start to relax, once she understood her environment. It was all part of her natural pattern for adapting fast, so she'd get a good night's sleep.

She'd flown in from her last house-sitting job in warm LA.

The new time zone, and the cold Pennsylvania mountain air, would take some getting used to.

She'd packed her warmest clothes, and her Sleepy-time tea, a jar of granulated honey, one can of chicken noodle soup, and her morning oatmeal, so she felt that she was prepared for anything.

It was important not to get sick, while adjusting to the colder climate. Her comfortable, familiar things would help her settle in better.

Breathing in the cold air, and watching Ginger sniff the trees, her thoughts turned to ways to stay warm.

Oatmeal for breakfast, which she'd have tomorrow morning, was a good way to start the day, and she'd have a cup of hot cocoa as well.

Beverly is not going to control everything I do.

I'll do the elf stuff, but only within reason. I decide what and when I eat.

She frowned, still bothered by the fact that her client had said little about the adorable little dog, who'd needed to go potty.

Ginger was now sniffing the trees, as if looking for something. Maybe she'd caught the scent of an animal.

"Poor little pup," Marcie said. "I'll bet she didn't let you out before she left." Marcie shook her head. "Well, don't worry. You and I are going to have lots of fun, and walks, and cuddles this Christmas."

Ginger turned to her and barked, then pulled on her leash, looking out past the trees, as if she wanted to go back into the wooded area.

"Do you want more of a walk?" Marcie asked. "We could go down the street a little bit. I don't think we should go into the woods."

The sky above the trees was growing dark, making the wooded area look darker as well. It would be night soon.

Marcie didn't want to venture too far when she didn't know the area yet.

Scanning the trees, she noted how remote they were here, with most houses empty and the shadows of the woods behind Beverly's house pressing in toward the house.

It gave her a brief, ominous feeling, as if something or someone was out there, and she shivered.

Ginger pulled on her leash and barked toward the woods.

What is she barking at? Scared little dog.

She remembered that King Charles Spaniels were not the bravest of dogs. The last one she had dog-sat seemed to hide from anything new. Ginger was likely similar.

Brushing the ominous feeling she'd had aside, she pulled back on the leash, trying to get Ginger to turn. "Come on, girl. We've got to go back inside. It's cold out here."

Ginger had probably scented something, like a deer or some other animal that had come into the wooded area behind the house. She was still interested in sniffing around that tree.

The taxi driver, who had driven Marcie out to the Large Bass Lake subdivision, which was a long way from the airport, had driven her straight to the house and had taken her on a lot of curves and turns on the mountain.

He'd had to slow down once and swerve when a deer jumped out in front of them.

According to the taxi driver, this was a frequent occurrence before deer hunting season.

There were simply too many deer, and these houses were close to the state game lands.

He'd warned her to wear something bright orange if she ventured into the trees around here, even if she was just in the back yard.

Neither she nor Ginger had anything orange to wear, and she didn't want to chance either of them getting shot, so they would not be going into the woods during her stay.

But even if it were not hunting season, she wasn't inclined to go traipsing into the woods alone anyway. She could turn an ankle, or worse, and then who would help her?

No, she would stick to the house and a hot cup of something in her favorite coffee mug to warm her.

Staying here was far different than staying in a city house.

Snow covered the ground and there were trees everywhere.

It reminded her of how isolated she would be if she got snowed in and that she should not put off stocking food in the house.

Ginger barked and pulled on the leash again, trying to go deeper into the woods, but Marcie bent down and, taking a dog biscuit from her pocket to distract the little dog, said, "Here, girl. I have a treat for you. A welcome gift."

The little dog turned once to look at her holding the biscuit and that's all it took to bring her running over to Marcie.

She took the biscuit, eating it right up.

Then she wagged her tail and looked up at Marcie, hopeful for more.

Marcie rubbed Ginger's ears. "Are you hungry? Let's go in and get warm again. Then we can both have a bite to eat."

The little dog wagged her tail and seemed happy to go back inside.

They went inside, the darkening woods behind them and Marcie feeling the cold on the back of her neck.

She shivered.

I need to remember to wear a scarf the next time I go outside.

And walks for Ginger need to happen before it's dark.

For the first time, she wondered if taking this job in such a remote area where she was alone with no neighbors, and might not see another person all day, had been such a great idea.

But she had taken the job, and the little dog was depending on her.

She looked down at Ginger and smiled.

Day two: The Elf watches you make breakfast.

WHEN MARCIE first arrived somewhere new, her routine was always the same: Chicken noodle soup for dinner and then oatmeal for breakfast, when she first arrived. Foods that were easy to travel with, fast to fix, and she could eat those things no matter how her stomach was feeling.

Her routine was full of her comfort foods.

Last night for dinner, she'd fixed the can of chicken noodle soup and found a packet of crackers in the kitchen.

She'd been jet-lagged, so after a shower and playing tug with Ginger, she'd put Ginger in her crate for the night and gone upstairs to settle into the big bed to read her book.

The mystery of who had killed a lawyer's secretary was just getting interesting when she heard tapping at the window and jumped.

Was someone outside? Knocking on the window?

Tap. Tap. Tap.

Her heart now racing, she laid the book down and slowly crept out of bed.

Moving slowly over to the window, she stood to the side of the window and looked out.

Seeing no one, her accelerated heartbeat started to slow.

There's no one out there.

Wind whistled through the trees suddenly and the branch which had been tapping at the window hit the window harder.

So that's what it was. Only a tree branch. There must be a storm moving in.

She wished the curtains were heavy drapes instead of sheers that showed if someone was inside the room.

But the room was on the second floor, and they would have to have a ladder to see in.

This is crazy. There's no one out there and there's no one in the neighbors' houses. I'm just letting the isolation get to me and I'm tired from the flight here.

Tomorrow everything will seem better.

Once she got back into bed and curled up in the warm spot she'd left, exhaustion took over and she fell asleep.

IN THE MORNING, her nervous reaction from the night before seemed silly.

A consequence of her being overly tired was what it was, and she determined to get to bed early and catch up on more sleep tonight. Plus, she really wanted to finish her book soon.

She stretched and yawned and then got out of bed and went over to her suitcase which she had not unpacked yet.

Routine was the fastest way to settle into a house and make it more her own in time for Christmas.

This time of year, especially, it was important to put her own touches on her temporary living space.

So, along with her usual things, she'd packed a few Christmassy things.

She had a new squeaky toy for Ginger's Christmas present. But she didn't want Ginger to see the long, multicolored caterpillar-looking toy with the big eyes yet.

She smiled at it, as she pulled a packet of oatmeal out of her suitcase. Then she changed into sweatpants and sweatshirt before heading downstairs.

Passing the elf on the kitchen table, she halted. "Creepy elf," she said. "I swear it looks like it's looking at me. Probably just my imagination because I don't like it."

She squinted at the elf. "Santa's elves should look happy. You do not look happy, Tananna."

That is a weird name, too. Who made up that creepy elf's name?

Bangs in her eyes, she appeared more like a petulant child than a happy elf. The pointy pale ears and snub nose could've been made to look friendlier.

"I wouldn't have one of those creepy elves in my house," she said. "If I find it creepy, I can just imagine how a little child might react. So what if it's an antique?"

Not everything from the past is worth keeping, acquiring, or hanging onto. Not everything from the past is good.

Marcie ought to know. She'd walked away from her past and had no plans to revisit it.

Her life was focused on today, and sometimes on tomorrow.

That kept good things present in her life because she believed in living in the present.

Yesterday was gone.

And there were no do-overs.

ZEKE WORKED in Manhattan and would be flying back and forth to Miami on the weekends, to spend time with Beverly.

She was excited for this Christmas vacation.

But for Zeke, his Christmas fun had begun already.

He'd had great fun playing with the elf, or rather playing with the camera he'd installed inside the elf. To make sure it worked, he'd tested it by sitting the elf in different places like the kitchen counter, the bathtub, a bed, and dresser to see what kind of angles he'd be able to see through the camera.

Then he'd helped Beverly draft some of the things that Marcie had been instructed to do.

He'd found Marcie Hayes purely by luck when she house-sat for his cousin, Harley, out in LA.

Young, blonde, beautiful, and with no living relatives to miss her, Marcie was perfect.

Now that all the pieces were in place, he sat back with a smile to watch the first video of Marcie meeting the elf and reading the letter.

He watched every expression on her face and listened to everything she said out loud.

It made him want to laugh.

Let the Christmas elf games begin.

AIR FORCE PILOT Ted Barr unloaded his gear from the back of the private plane he'd flown in, to the Poconos, after he'd let his dog out.

His buddy, Nathan, now out of the Air Force, had his own plane to do charter flights and had offered him a ride.

"Thanks, Nathan," he said to the redheaded pilot.

Ted's Golden Retriever, Ace, waited patiently by his side, tail wagging.

"No worries," Nathan said. "It was on my way. Enjoy your holiday at your new place."

"Thanks. I will. You, too. Tell Sharon hello and Merry Christmas from me."

Nathan and Sharon were old friends whom he'd met while stationed on Okinawa. Nathan was on his way to Upstate New York, where Sharon's aunt lived.

He'd be picking her aunt up and bringing her back to stay for the holidays with them.

The timing for Ted to ride up to the Poconos with Nathan had worked out perfectly.

"Will do." Nathan clasped Ted's hand. "Merry Christmas. If you change your mind about spending the holiday alone, call me."

Ted nodded and said, "I will," then turned to Ace. "Come on, boy." He walked toward the airport office, Ace trotting along beside him, as the plane taxied down the runway to take off.

Inside the office, a woman named Shirley gave him the keys to a Chevy Blazer.

He thanked her and headed out toward the vehicle. He

loaded his bags and let Ace climb in, then he got in, started the vehicle, and headed toward his new house in the Large Bass Lake subdivision of the Pocono Mountains.

Since his weekend date, Heather, had cancelled two days before they were supposed to leave, he'd decided to move on.

There was no reason he couldn't hit the slopes without her.

Things were over with Heather. He'd felt it, even before she'd called to confirm that hunch. So, it had come as less of a surprise. He was ready to end things as well.

He would break in his new house without a girlfriend to sweeten the time, but he had Ace for company.

It wasn't like he'd be alone for Christmas.

His family wasn't used to spending Christmas together any more, since both sons had joined the military.

Often, Ted was wherever the Air Force sent him, while his twin brother, Jack Barr, a Marine, was away on a mission.

Having both sons home at the same time was rare for his parents. Though each would get leave, it wasn't always at the same time, or even at Christmas.

Now that their parents had retired, they'd begun to travel.

His twin brother, Jack, would be off on his honeymoon this year, and their parents were going off on their first cruise, a trip that had been at the top of his father's bucket list.

Ted was stationed at Seymour Johnson AFB and had moved off base into a rented mobile home after Ace came into his life. The Golden Retriever was his constant companion, and his next-door neighbor watched the dog when Ted had to be away.

Ted had just bought his first house, agreeing with his

parents that at thirty-three it was time for him to set roots down somewhere; he'd picked a house in ski country.

The house was an investment, and a vacation home. If he wasn't using it, he could rent it out. As the house was in the Poconos, he'd have no trouble renting it.

Weather predicted good snowfall tonight. That could mean good skiing in a day or two. In the meantime, he had supplies to get in and a house to check out and make his own.

After Ace finished sniffing all the things in the house that interested him, which was pretty much every inch and every corner, the Golden Retriever settled onto the floor next to the fireplace to watch Ted.

MARCIE TOOK her oatmeal out of the microwave, after she let Ginger outside. As cold as it was, she doubted the little dog would want to stay outside longer than necessary.

The oatmeal would warm Marcie, and then she would bundle herself and the little dog up to go for a walk.

She'd seen a cute sweater for the little dog in the room with the crate that Ginger slept in.

Eyeing the elf on the table, she held up her warm bowl and said, "See? I'm having oatmeal for breakfast. Your owner left no food in the house, so you don't get any big breakfasts around here, until I can go to the grocery store. That will just have to do."

She nodded at the elf, and then moved to let Ginger back in, before sitting at the kitchen table to eat her breakfast.

The minute Marcie sat at the table to eat; Ginger started barking at the elf.

"You really hate that thing, don't you?" Marcie said.

Ginger jumped and put her front paws on Marcie's legs, then barked again.

Marcie reached a hand down to scratch her ears. "All right. I'll start putting the thing away, since it upsets you so much. Come on, we'll find a place for it."

Zeke watched the video of Marcie with her oatmeal. She wore sweatpants and a sweatshirt, which hid everything but her curves. There was no hiding those.

He enjoyed the view of her ass as she stood in front of the microwave.

The sweats clung to her curves, making him wish he could run his hands over them.

Then she turned, and started talking to the elf.

She's defiant. Eating her oatmeal and standing up to the directions. I wonder how much of a fighter she is, and what it will take to make her compliant.

She was talking to the elf. As if it could hear her. She had no idea.

It could not only hear her, but it could also see her.

He laughed.

Then Ginger was barking again.

Bark, bark, bark.

That damn dog hated him, and the elf too.

Zeke would be happy if he never had to hear that little dog barking at him again.

Perhaps someday that could be arranged if he ended up staying with Beverly.

She was useful to him, so it was worth keeping her happy and staying with her.

But that didn't mean something couldn't happen to the little dog, one day down the road.

He could tell Marcie had picked up the elf and was moving it somewhere.

But where?

The camera angle showed the rooms as she moved through them, and then he heard a door opening slowly.

The front closet door.

Marcie lifted the elf and set it down on the top shelf.

"You can live in the closet," Marcie said.

Then she closed the door, and the video went dark.

"Son of a bitch!" Zeke stood, yelling. "She's locked it in the closet."

Now I won't see anything until she takes it back out.

He needed to borrow Beverly's phone to send the house sitter a message.

Or get Beverly to do it, which would be easier, since she was in Miami, and he was in Manhattan.

It was a two-hour drive to Beverly's ski chalet in the Pocono Mountains.

The camera would stay inside the elf as planned even though right now he couldn't control where Marcie put the elf.

Calming down, he realized she would have to get it out of the closet to take selfies with it.

If she followed the directions she'd been given, that would happen once a day.

He would try to be patient and wait.

TED'S HOUSE WAS EMPTY, except for a couch, a bed, and the dining room table with six chairs that had been delivered yesterday.

His realtor had met the deliverymen, and had overseen the furniture set up, and then left Ted final copies of the paperwork along with another business card and a note to call if he needed anything.

He had a long list of things to buy to make the house more comfortable, but this was a start.

At some point, he'd have someone over to celebrate the purchase of his first home, but for now, he was content just to be here with Ace.

They'd been inside for too long though and he knew Ace needed to go out for some exercise.

While that applied to his dog, it applied to Ted too.

Ted reached for the black leather leash that had Ace's name on it. "Ready, Ace?"

The seven-year-old Golden Retriever wagged his tail, and came over to Ted. He stood still as Ted put his leash on.

After clipping the leash on, Ted scratched Ace's ear. "Good boy," he said.

Ace wagged his tail even harder.

Ted pulled on his winter gloves and opened the door. Cold air blew in as they went out. He closed and locked the door.

A new flat screen TV was being delivered today, so he wouldn't walk Ace far.

He wanted to be able to see the house in case the delivery guy came early.

The air outside was cool and crisp, but not overly cold, like it could be in December. Sun shining on the snow made it sparkle.

This would've been a perfect day for skiing. Tomorrow I will do just that.

He couldn't wait to hit the slopes and try out new hills and trails.

He walked down the steps with Ace and headed out for their morning walk.

Not far from his house, he saw a young woman with long, straight, silky blonde hair, wearing a thick, off-white cowl neck sweater with a pink scarf and mittens, but no coat. She caught his gaze, and his interest.

She was holding back a very excited King Charles Spaniel on a leash.

The pretty brown-and-white spaniel looked well cared for and was perhaps spoiled.

He was clearly witnessing a power struggle between the two, to determine who was the alpha.

"Slow down, Ginger. It's slippery here," the woman said, her voice drifting Ted's way, like snow falling.

Her voice was soft and sweet, though she sounded exasperated, which made him smile.

She had the kind of voice a man would enjoy listening to.

A light dusting of snow was falling all around, as the wind blew, making the snow swirl in the air in a circular dance.

The woman's boots slid on the snow as she shuffled her feet fast to keep her footing.

She didn't fall, though she might have.

The excitable little dog she was walking didn't listen to her at all.

It was as if the little dog was in charge.

Ted gave a brief shake of his head.

If you're going to have a dog, you must know there's only one alpha.

The pretty lady needs to take her dog to obedience class, so she can learn how to take command of her dog.

Nothing about her is authoritative.

No wonder the little dog isn't listening.

Ginger insisted on sniffing everything she came across and running around with her tail wagging, while the woman laughed and called her back.

He had to admit Ginger was a cute little dog.

The woman wasn't bad, either. She was pretty in a refreshing way.

He wished he could see beneath the mittens, to her ring finger, to find out if she was engaged, or married.

AT FIRST, Marcie didn't notice the tall, handsome man walking the dog.

He and his dog were both quiet. He was much taller than Marcie, who was only five foot five with her shoes on.

A two-day growth of beard, and a dark mustache gave the man a rugged look.

Well, hello, Mr. TDH.

Tall, dark, and handsome men were her favorites.

Not only because heroes in the old fairytales she'd loved as a child were tall, dark, and handsome, but because they were the knights and princes who were defenders of women and children.

That was the part she liked best.

If she were honest, she still loved those stories.

With his dark, wavy hair in a military cut, Mr. Tall, Dark, and Handsome had an air of command and authority.

Likely, he was the take charge type.

He certainly is in command of his dog.

What a good dog.

I wish I had better command of Ginger. Of course, we just met. Maybe things will get better.

She liked to think positively.

The little dog was so energetic it made it hard to walk her, and the slippery ice and snow weren't helping.

They were two streets over from the house she was staying at, which was in a cul-de-sac at the edge of the development, with tall trees in the back yard.

Suddenly, instead of each checking the other out, while they paid attention to their dogs, Ted and Marcies eyes met and held, as if magnetized toward each other.

There was something there. Some spark between them.

"Hello," he said.

"Hello," she answered.

"I'm Ted Barr, your new neighbor." He pointed to his house. "Just bought this place."

His attention went back on the dogs, who were sniffing each other. "And this is Ace," he said.

"Nice to meet you," she said. "I'm Marcie, and this is Ginger."

"Nice to meet you, Marcie," he said. "And Ginger. Looks like you're having trouble with her."

"Yes, well, we're not used to each other," she said. "I'm dog-sitting and this is only day two. We're still getting to know each other."

"A dog-sitter, I'll have to keep that in mind," Ted said. "Do you have a card?"

"Oh yes," she said. Taking the end of one of her mittens with her teeth, she pulled it off, and then reached into her jeans and pulled out a slightly crumpled business card.

She handed it to him.

He glanced down at the card.

Home Sweet Home House-Sitting Services.

Ted smiled.

Great. It's got her phone number on it, which means I can call her and ask her out.

"Nice," he said. "So, does the dog live in this subdivision, or do you?"

"The dog lives here, for now, while her owner is away," she smiled at him.

Ginger woofed and Marcie bent down to scratch her ears.

"The rest of the time, she lives in New York City. I'm just keeping her company through the Christmas holidays."

"This is a great place to visit," he said. "It's beautiful here."

"Yes, it is." She nodded.

"This is ski country," he said. "Do you ski?"

"Oh, no." She shook her head. "I've never ..."

Ginger yapped at her, wanting to move on down the road.

"... skied," she finished.

"Plenty of time to learn," Ted said. "Think about it."

"I've got to go," Marcie said."

"Be careful on that ice," he said.

"I will," she said.

Ginger was now pulling on her leash for Marcie to follow her.

Marcie put her mitten back on and, following the little dog, waved goodbye to Ted and Ace.

He's as nice as he is handsome. And so easy to talk to.

She would've liked to have talked longer, to get to know him better.

Maybe I'll see him again, later.

Since she'd be house-sitting and dog-sitting all month, there was plenty of time to bump into him again.

I'd better take Ginger back to the house, and then head to the grocery store.

Everything seems so remote here, but with this many houses, surely a grocery store isn't far.

Ginger has had plenty of exercise this morning and should be good for a while. I'll need to check her paws and make sure they are dry.

Back at the house, Marcie dried Ginger's paws with a towel, and then fired up the laptop she's brought with her.

Five minutes later, much to her surprise, she learned that the closest grocery store was thirty minutes away. The closest gas station was also thirty minutes away.

It seemed everything was.

Being on top of a mountain was different from anywhere she'd lived before.

"Well, we won't be walking to the grocery, Ginger," she said. "And I'd better stock up when I go tonight, in case we get snowed in."

The little dog wagged her tail and barked. Then she placed her head on Marcie's lap, and looked up at her with her big, brown eyes.

"Who could resist those eyes," she asked the little dog, as she rubbed Ginger's ears, enjoying how soft the dog's fur was.

"I'd take you with me, but I don't want to leave you in a cold car. That's no good," she said. "And I can't take you into the store. But I'll make a good list before I leave, and I won't dilly-dally. We can play when I get back."

Ginger leaned into her hand and seemed happy.

Marcie had to remind herself the little dog was used to

her owner being at work all day. So she shouldn't feel bad about leaving just to go to the grocery.

Ginger would get plenty of attention while Marcie was staying with her.

Marcie texted the picture she'd taken for day two's picture to Beverly, which was one of the elf holding a spoon and a bowl of oatmeal.

Beverly immediately texted back.

No. No. No. You were supposed to cook a big breakfast and take the elf pic doing that. Not eating boring oatmeal. Go read my note again.

Marcie texted back. *No can do. There's no food in the house. All I had for breakfast was the oatmeal I brought with me.*

Beverly texted. *Food is not included in your compensation. You'll have to go to the store and then make another breakfast and take the picture I told you to take! You can fix it for dinner, no one will know the difference. But I need that pic!*

Marcie rolled her eyes before texting back. *I didn't expect food as compensation. Had already planned to go to the store today.*

Marcie dropped her phone in her bag. She was done texting today.

She'd already told Beverly more than she needed to.

It's really none of her business.

Beverly had put her on the defensive and into explaining mode.

That didn't need to happen again.

Stuffing the long shopping list into her bag, she bundled up to head out the door for the thirty-minute drive to the small town nearby.

When she was inside the grocery, she rounded a corner, and nearly bumped into Ted.

"Well, hello," he said.

"Hello," she answered. "Are you baking?"

He glanced down at his cart.

Flour, sugar, salt and pepper, butter, and other basics were in his cart. It did look like he could be baking.

"Stocking my house for the first time," he said. "There's nothing in the house but empty cabinets."

"Oh, wow," she said. "There's not much in the house I'm staying in either, but there are spices and things like that."

"Sounds like we both need to stock up, in case of a storm," he said.

"Yes, and I need to hurry and get back to Ginger," she said.

She would love to stay longer, talking to him, but she really did need to get going.

"Okay, neighbor," Ted said. "I'm just down the road if you need anything." He pulled a piece of paper out of his pocket, jotted his number down, and handed it to her. "Here's my number. Don't hesitate to call."

"Thanks," she said, taking the paper and putting it in her purse. "I will." She took hold of her cart again. "Better get back to shopping. See you later."

"Later," he replied with a nod, and then watched her hurry down the aisle to finish her shopping.

Marcie arrived home, let Ginger out right away, and then carried the groceries in. She had enough for two weeks.

Surely, if they did get snowed in, it wouldn't be longer than that. And her neighbor Ted wasn't far away.

She felt much safer, knowing there was someone nearby that she could call.

House-sitting in the Poconos was much different than in a city. Much more isolating.

That was something to keep in mind the next time she

was offered a job, and the question to ask was: How remote is it?

The house was eerily quiet without Ginger barking.

Marcie was happy to let Ginger back in.

She didn't feel like cooking a real dinner, which could take a while, and breakfast was sounding not half bad right now, as a replacement. Plus she could cook it and get that darn photo for day two over with.

That would get Beverly off her back.

Her phone, which she'd set on vibrate, had been going off all through the grocery store.

She hadn't needed to look, more than twice, to know who was blowing up her phone with text after text.

There was no point looking at them. She'd take the picture and send it, and then she would look at the texts and delete them all.

CHAPTER 3

*M*arcie watched the snow falling outside the bedroom window from beneath the warmth of her covers. She didn't feel like getting out of bed and facing the cold.

It was like when she had been a small girl and didn't want to get ready for the school bus.

Now that she was an adult, and managing her own time, with her new lifestyle, she did not have to get out of bed yet.

Somehow that made it all the harder.

The fireplace heater in the living room downstairs had long since gone out, and now all the rooms were cold.

Even her bedroom had a chill, and if she so much as moved beneath the covers, cold sheets would touch her feet.

It was past time to get up.

Living on top of a mountain, in snow and ski country, was a new experience for Marcie.

She had to learn how to use the wood-stove in a way that the house wouldn't be freezing in the morning when she woke.

She wondered if the stack of wood beside the front

porch would last through her stay. She would be here for a month. If she needed more wood to heat the house, she wasn't sure where to get it, or how much it would cost her.

The house had electric heat, but there was a locked thermostat box, and she didn't know where the key was.

Beverly had said nothing about it, or the wood on the porch. There was also nothing in their initial conversation about utilities.

That had been a mistake. One she wouldn't make again.

She would have to ask Beverly where the key was.

The only written directions had been about the elf contest.

Marcie went to check the list again, to remind herself of what she was supposed to do with the elf today.

She read the list again and groaned.

Day three: Elf puts up the Christmas tree with your help.

"That sounds like a lot of work," she told Ginger.

The little dog looked up at her and woofed.

Today Beverly wants me to put the tree up, and that could be festive, so I might as well get to it. I like Christmas trees, so it will be nice to have one.

The cheerful greens and reds of Christmas would cheer up the stark white of the snow outside and the dark woods, which had brought a gloom to her normally cheerful mood this morning which was far from Christmassy.

Almost everything inside the house was wood, with lots of brown, and not one cheerful color anywhere.

All very rustic, but the cold of the house was making it feel bleak.

She needed warmth and some color to brighten her mood.

Marcie bundled up and took Ginger outside, waiting for her to do her business.

On the way back in, she carried more wood inside for the fire.

Maybe my new friend, Ted, will know where to get wood for the fireplace or have an idea of how much I'll need during my stay here.

If it were nice out, she would take Ginger for a walk to Ted's house, knock on his door, and ask.

It took her a while to get a fire started, but after she had a good one going, she headed downstairs to the basement, where Beverly's Christmas things were stored.

Climbing up and down the stairs, carrying boxes, was sure to warm her up and get her blood moving.

Each box was clearly marked with a list of everything inside. There were also instructions for how Beverly wanted the decorations to be put up.

So particular and she's not even here to see it.

Then Marcie remembered she had to share the elf photos.

Oh wait, this will all be shared online, where everyone will see them, so maybe that's why she's being particular about the tree.

Marcie cut her some slack and then went about getting everything into the living room for the tree to go up.

As she attempted to carry the first big box up the stairs, Ginger kept getting under foot and wouldn't listen.

Marcie put the box down and took Ginger upstairs to put her in her crate.

Ginger immediately gave her the stink eye. She clearly was not happy about it.

Marcie ignored Ginger's mood and went back downstairs for the big Christmas tree box.

Dang these things are hard to manage.

She had to keep pausing with it, to rest.

It wasn't so much that the box was super heavy, as it was large and awkward. And she didn't want to fall on the stairs.

Finally, after lugging the box all the way up the stairs, she rested at the top.

Marcie continued through Ginger's room, into the hall, and up the three steps into the living room.

The little dog was now pouting with her head resting on her paws, as she laid in her crate watching Marcie.

"Oh, those eyes," Marcie said with a laugh. "What a look you are giving me!"

She made the trip several times, with boxes.

"I'm getting my exercise today, Ginger," she said, after climbing the stairs again.

The little dog was clearly still pouting.

"If you would have helped me, or at least stayed out of my way, instead of getting under foot, I wouldn't have put you in there."

Ginger gave Marcie a look.

She was so expressive, Marcie couldn't help but laugh.

"You sure are giving me the stink eye," she said. "What an expression! Once everything is in the living room, I'll let you back out. I promise."

The look Ginger was giving Marcie didn't change. Though her crate was her place, right now the little dog wanted out, but she was still pouting too much to ask.

"Are you holding a little grudge against me now?" Marcie asked.

Marcie had put Ginger in her crate and not let her run around loose while she handled the big box, and that's when the pouting began.

It was hard to look at her little face, because looking at her made Marcie feel guilty.

The little dog didn't move her head or thump her tail.

"My, but you're put out with me." Marcie laughed. "But that look is not going to work. I'm not going to risk tumbling down those stairs, and breaking something, even if you are cute, adorable, and giving me that look. But I'll be done soon, and then you can come out to play."

Marcie had to make one more trip downstairs for the last box.

Ginger tipped her head to the side. Her tail lifted and thumped once.

The only enthusiasm she summoned.

Once Marcie had hauled everything up the stairs and let the little dog out again, hopefully all would be forgiven.

By the time she'd brought everything into the living room, she was thirsty, so she went into the kitchen, made a cup of herbal tea, and then carried it and a few crackers into the living room where she placed it all on an end table before going to let Ginger out.

Ginger was happy to be out, but she was still mad at Marcie and ignored her.

She ran up the stairs into the living room and started sniffing around the tree.

"I doubt it has a scent," Marcie said. "Fake trees don't. But sniff away, my little friend."

Ginger finished sniffing the tree and, not seeing anything else of interest, came back over to Marcie, who was sitting on the couch sipping her tea and eating a cracker.

"Oh, now you want to be friends again," Marcie laughed. "But I think you just love me for my cracker."

She laughed again and gave Ginger half a cracker.

After a few good ear scratches and part of a cracker, the little dog settled down next to Marcie on the couch.

"I'm glad you're not still mad at me," she said, "because I'm enjoying your company. I'm not so sure house-sitting somewhere this remote again would be a good idea, completely alone. In the city, it's easy to go out for a coffee or a glass of wine and not feel isolated. But here on top of the mountain, where would you go? And where would you find any people?"

They sat for a few moments, cuddling, as Ginger gave her an occasional lick on her hand.

"Well, what do you think, Ginger?" she asked. "Should I decorate the tree according to Beverly's detailed instructions, or do it my way?"

Ginger looked at her and woofed once.

"I can't tell which way you're voting, Ginger, but I'm voting for my way. Since this is the beginning of December and we're the ones who must look at this tree all month. She won't even see the tree; other than the picture I send her."

The instructions on the boxes said the homeowner wanted all the decorations put away before she got home.

That was fine.

Ginger licked Marcie's hand again.

Marcie smiled. "I love you too, girl."

Ginger was easy to love.

Unlike some humans which took more effort.

A good dog gave the kind of love unmatched by any human.

"The instructions from your owner are so irritating," Marcie said. "I wish that elf was a nice elf, a real elf who could actually help me." Marcie sighed. "Cooking, baking, or decorating. It's on me to do it all. But, that's okay. I'd just as soon leave that creepy elf in the closet, until I have to take a picture of it."

Ginger woofed once.

Marcie took that as a yes.

"I know you don't like that old elf either," Marcie said. "We're in agreement on that. What a weird gift for a boyfriend to give. Or maybe not, if he did it to help Beverly win the contest. Five thousand dollars is nothing to sneeze at."

Marcie, having finished her tea and crackers, set the teacup down and stood up.

Time to put the tree together.

The tree had four sections and was tall … and fat. Luckily, the sections were all marked, because without the markings, she felt it would have been confusing trying to put it together.

Even with those, she still struggled getting all the pieces connected, but finally got it done.

It stood in the middle of the room.

Then she took all the liquor bottles off the rolling cart in the corner and carried them into the kitchen.

It wasn't like she'd be entertaining.

The bottles could sit on the kitchen counter, in the corner, and she'd store the rolling cart out of the way, maybe in Ginger's room.

Then the big tree could go in the corner.

She carried the rolling cart down the three steps and into the room past the kitchen, where Ginger's crate was, as Ginger followed.

"I think it will be all right in here, don't you?" she asked the little dog, who wagged her tail. "I'll bet you miss having someone to talk to you all day when Beverly is at work. So maybe having a dog-sitter is a happy thing because you'll get more attention."

Ginger woofed once.

"I'll take that as a yes," Marcie said.

"Okay, well, come on. We have a great big tree to decorate and then a pretty picture to take. I'm not talking about the one with the ugly elf. I'm going to take a pretty picture, just for me."

Ginger followed her out of the room and up the three small steps into the living room.

First, Marcie checked the strings of lights to make sure they all worked. Though everything looked new, she didn't want to have to unstring the lights if she put them up without checking and then found some or all of the bulbs didn't work.

She strung the lights on the tree and plugged them in after she was finished.

"There," she said, stepping back to look at the tree. "I prefer white lights, but colorful ones are cheerful."

Marcie sat on the floor, scratching Ginger's ears and looking where she might place the bulbs and other decorations. She wasn't going to do the tree Beverly's way, counting out this many of this bulb and that many of that one.

That's much too anal. Marcie shook her head.

Decorating should be about how things look and how they make you feel, not about counting how many of each color thing hangs on the tree.

It isn't as if the bulbs have any sentimental significance, like this many red bulbs for children and that many gold bulbs for grandchildren. Like the jewelry some women wear, with this many of one color of stones for kids and that many of another color for grandkids.

Something like that might make sense to count colored bulbs.

No, this is more about Beverly's need to control every detail of every little thing.

I'm not letting her control me. I'll decorate this tree the way I want to. I'm the one who must look at the tree all month. If I do it my way, I will enjoy looking at it.

Marcie would've skipped the whole elf thing and stuck that creepy elf in a closet for good, not looking at it again, if she'd had her way.

But she did understand wanting to win the money. So she'd go along with Beverly, to help her win.

Maybe they would win and then the woman would give her a better bonus if she was feeling generous.

Though Marcie wouldn't count on that.

She'd learned people could surprise you with being generous, but they could also surprise you with being stingy.

Only time would tell.

Now that she'd finished the tree, it was time to take the elf picture.

Marcie went to open the closet, where the elf sat on the top shelf.

The elf still creeped her out because she felt like its eyes followed her. But she picked it up anyway and brought it down from the shelf.

She had her phone in her hand and turned to head for the tree.

The minute Ginger saw that she had the elf, she started barking at it.

Marcie set the elf in the branches, making it look as if the elf held a string of lights.

Ginger stood behind her, still barking, and then she gave a low growl.

"Wow. You really don't like that elf," Marcie said. "Tell

you what. I'll put it back in the coat closet when we're done, okay?"

Ginger kept barking at it.

Marcie knew Ginger wasn't going to quit barking until the elf was put away. So, she took the picture as quickly as she could and then took the elf off the tree. She opened the coat closet and stowed it on the top shelf again and closed the door.

"There," she said. "That creepy elf is locked away until we let her out again for the next picture. She'll live there till picture time. I don't blame you, Ginger. I don't like her, either."

Ginger gave one last bark at the closed door, as if to tell the elf to stay in there and not come out, and then she was quiet again.

It had grown dark outside, though it wasn't nighttime.

Marcie went to the window to look out and see what the weather was doing.

Heavy clouds blocked the sun, making it dark. Snow was falling.

She was glad she'd gone to the store earlier. They might get snowed in, but she had food, water, and dog food. Enough for two weeks. They would be fine.

"Come on, Ginger, let's go out in the snow!" she called to the little dog. "You need the exercise, and it will be fun to catch a snowflake on my tongue!"

The little dog leaped off the couch and started jumping around and woofing at Marcie. She knew what 'go out' meant.

"Okay, I'm getting ready," Marcie said. "Just need my coat and boots."

Ginger excitedly danced around barking, until Marcie opened the door of the closet.

She felt rather than saw Ginger take a fierce guard-dog stance behind her, as Ginger started to growl at the elf.

"It's okay, girl," she said. "I'll grab them quick and close the door again. That elf isn't getting out, until I take her out for picture time."

She closed the door right away, but Ginger didn't change her stance or attitude, until Marcie had her coat and boots on and went to get Ginger's leash.

Then all was well again and Ginger wagged her tail, happy to be going out.

LOOKING ONLINE, Ted discovered that the only furniture and department stores near his house in Gouldsboro, Pennsylvania, were an hour away in Scranton.

If that was where everyone had to go to buy things, then that was where he'd have to go.

This was part of living in a remote area on top of a mountain, so he'd need to get used to it.

Ted decided it was too cold to leave Ace waiting in a vehicle, so he left him at home. He had a long list of things to buy from sheets and blankets to dishes and silverware.

He planned to stock the house for six in case his whole family came.

Now that his brother, Jack, was getting married this month they'd be two, Ted's mom and dad made four, while adding Ted and a girl made six.

If a set of anything came with eight, he'd buy it, but otherwise he was planning for six.

This kind of shopping wasn't something Ted had ever done before, but the sales clerks were more than happy to help him.

"Just no flowery stuff," he told them.

Too many designs were flowery.

But he didn't like the stark black-and-white look either.

"I don't care if this is what is in. It's too gloomy, like going to a funeral. I'm furnishing a ski chalet; everything should be about relaxing while on vacation."

He ended up with blue things, blue being a color he liked, which was neither flowery and girlie nor stark.

At the last store, as he purchased items, Marcie's card fell out of his wallet.

He started thinking about her, as he picked the card up.

He wanted to ask her out and now he had her number in his hand.

She didn't ski but he could teach her.

Everyone who stayed in ski country should try it. At least once.

In his Welcome to the Poconos folder, from his real estate agent, there'd been a few fliers from Montage Mountain with lift ticket prices and a schedule.

I'll ask her if she'd like to go skiing with me, before I fly to Montana.

Maybe she'll keep an eye on Ace for me while I'm gone. She could let him out and feed him. That would be better than putting him in a kennel. He's already adapting to our new home.

He'd left Ace at home, this time, because he was stocking the cabin which might fill the Blazer, plus there was all the waiting in the car.

I'll call her right now.

He got out his cell phone and dialed.

"Hello?" her soft melodic voice answered.

Hers was a voice he could listen to all night.

"Hello, Marcie," he said. "This is Ted. I have a couple of things to ask you."

"Oh. Hello, Ted," she said. "It's nice to hear from you. Ask away."

"First, I was wondering if you could watch Ace when I fly to Montana to be in my brother's wedding. It's this month, while you're still here."

"Sure," she said. "I can do that."

"Great! I really appreciate it."

"You haven't asked my price," she said.

"That's right, I haven't," he said. "What do you charge?"

"Forty dollars for a full day, twenty-five for a thirty-minute visit, overnight is seventy-five."

"Ace will need to be fed and let out to play. He doesn't need around-the-clock attention and pampering, but he does need exercise. And he's met you already."

"A few more meet-ups and we'll be best buddies," she said.

"Dogs love you," he said.

"And I love them," she said.

"Ace is used to me going away for days, but I'll only be gone for a weekend this time. Mom and Dad have watched him before and they say he's mopey the first couple days. By the time he gets over being mopey this time, I'll be back. I'd rather have you look after him, so I don't have to put him in a kennel."

"Okay," she said. "How many days?"

"I fly out on the thirteenth and back on the fifteenth. It's a short out and back."

"Great. When do you want to do our first meet-up?"

Was that hopefulness in her voice? Wanting to meet soon?

"That leads me to my second question," He said. "Would you like to go skiing with me, this weekend? I thought we could try out Montage Mountain."

"Have you skied there before?" she asked.

"Yes," he said. "Several times when I was younger. My whole family skis."

"It sounds like you have an active family," she said.

"I do."

"I'm not athletic, but I took dance classes as a child," she said.

"Dancers are athletes, too. What type of dance?"

"Ballet, jazz, tap."

"You'll love skiing," he said. "They have beginner classes at Montage Mountain, or I could teach you."

"I've heard skiing is expensive," she said. "I'm not sure I can afford it."

"Since I'm asking you on a date, I'll pay," he said. "Don't worry about the expense. It will be fun. If you want to go out with me."

"Yes, I'd love to go out with you," she said, her breath rushing out fast.

He heard her voice change. They were off to a good beginning.

"Great. So, Friday then."

"Yes," she said. "I'll see you then."

"See you then. We're going to get more snow before Friday, so it should be good skiing by then. Did you get everything you needed at the store in case we get a heavy snow?"

"Yes. I'm good for several weeks if I can't get out."

"Good. If you need anything before Friday, or any time, call me. Remember I'm just down the road."

"Okay," she said. "I will."

It sounded as if she didn't want to hang up.

"Is everything all right over at your place?"

"Yes," she said. "All good."

"Great," he said. "Talk soon."

"Yes. Talk soon," she replied and then softly hung up the phone.

He smiled at his phone.

She didn't want to hang up. That was a good sign.

Day four: Watch a Christmas DVD with the elf...

MARCIE LOOKED OUTSIDE AT ALL the snow which had fallen the night before.

I'll have to shovel a path for Ginger to do her business, and another path for me to get to the car.

She moved away from the window and over to the elf contest to-do list on the refrigerator.

We're not doing a DVD today, instead we're doing the elf shoveling snow, which isn't supposed to be until later.

Beverly is not in charge of snow falling. So, we're going with the snow while we have it.

She took a pen and crossed the Christmas movie idea off and then wrote: Elf shovels snow. Build snowman?

I'll switch this elf schedule around and get the elf shoveling snow part out of the way.

We can watch a DVD another time.

She bundled up, and then let Ginger out.

Ginger stood just outside the door, likely needing to go but with nowhere to do it. The snow that had fallen was up to her belly.

Marcie grabbed a shovel. "Don't worry, girl. I'll clear you a path as fast as I can. If you must go before I get it done, just go."

The little dog looked up at her with pleading eyes, and then looked at the snow, and barked at it several times.

"The snow might be cold on your paws right now," Marcie said, "but you need to go. I'll dry your paws off with a warm towel after we go back inside."

Ginger woofed again.

Marcie started shoveling, putting her back into it, and after about twenty minutes had a path to the tree that Ginger liked to pee beside. "There you go, girl," she said.

The little dog hurried to the tree and did her business so fast that Marcie knew she'd been desperately holding it in.

"Good girl," Marcie said. "Now we can go in. Come on."

They headed back inside the warm house.

Marcie pulled off her wet boots and mittens and then her scarf and coat. She left them in the kitchen, where drips from the melting snow on the floor wouldn't ruin anything.

"Okay, Ginger, you're next," she said. Then she stepped into the guest bathroom beside the kitchen and grabbed a towel.

Turning the oven on, she set it to three fifty and waited for the oven to heat.

After it was heated, she put the towel inside. After a few minutes, when it was warm, she took the towel out and said, "Here, girl."

Ginger had been licking her paws, but she got up and came over to Marcie.

Marcie took one paw and wrapped the towel around it. Taking each paw, she made sure there was no snow or ice stuck in Ginger's toe pads or on her fur.

Soon Ginger was warm and dry, wagging her tail, and giving Marcie hand licks.

Marcie laughed and bent down close to Ginger's face. "You know that tickles."

Ginger promptly licked her on the nose.

Laughing so hard that she almost fell over backward; Marcie gave Ginger a hug. "You and I do have fun, don't we?"

Ginger woofed.

"Okay, girl. I'm going to go make some tea to warm up, and I need to eat my oatmeal." She scratched Ginger's ear who leaned into her for more, which made Marcie smile.

She was growing to love this little dog and it was going to be hard when it was time to say goodbye to her.

This was the hardest part of dog-sitting.

She couldn't have her own dog, because she moved around too much, so she loved everyone else's.

Sometimes that was hard if she got too attached.

"After I have breakfast, I'll go back outside and shovel a way out to the car and a way for the car to get out. You can stay inside." She glanced out the window. "I wonder how soon the snowplow will come. Or if they even have one here."

Ginger stood next to her, looking out the sliding glass doors.

"At some point, we're going to have to take a picture of that elf out there, holding the snow shovel. But that can wait."

She moved to open the cabinet where the bowls were, but as she opened the door, she saw the elf sitting on the stack of bowls, its elf face inches from her own.

She screamed, slammed the cabinet door closed, and jumped back, shaking.

The elf had moved! It had moved!

She took a deep breath.

No, it couldn't have. I put it in the front closet yesterday and closed the door.

With a shaking hand, she slowly pulled the cabinet door open again and peered inside.

Tananna, the creepy antique elf, was sitting on the stack of bowls staring back at her.

Suddenly Marcie's mouth was very dry. She was no longer hungry. And she had the feeling that someone had been in the house last night and moved the doll.

Ginger was there, beside her now, and, as soon as she spotted the antique elf, had taken up barking at it.

A more ferocious sound than Marcie had heard her make before.

She turned and ran through the house, room by room, checking every door and window.

All locked. No one had gotten in.

But wait! The key!

She fumbled with the front door lock and yanked the door open to see if the key was still beneath the mat.

CHAPTER 4

Marcie bent down and pushed the snow away, before lifting the mat. Would the key be there?

Yes.

The silver key laid right in front of her, and she picked it up, as she frowned, thinking.

If someone had gotten in, all that snow would have been disturbed. But it wasn't.

It didn't appear that anyone had broken in.

But if no one had, then how did that elf get moved?

She put the key back for the darn cleaning lady who never had contacted her, and who might never come to clean, and then closed and locked the front door again.

Feeling shaky, she entered the kitchen again, saw Ginger still barking at the elf, and suddenly she got so mad about the whole thing that she grabbed the elf and flung it to the floor.

"Here, Ginger! Have a new chew toy."

Maybe the dog would tear it up and then Marcie could

tell Beverly that they were done with the contest, because her dog had eaten the elf contestant.

Though it didn't look like that was going to happen.

Ginger, frightened by the creepy thing, was now hiding under a kitchen chair, growling at the elf. Too scared to attack the elf, but not too scared to bark and growl at it.

Great. Well, that sudden idea isn't going to work.

Leaving the elf on the floor where she'd flung it, Marcie decided to make herself some tea to warm up.

Her fingers were chilled, from her digging through the snow at the front door without wearing gloves, and she needed something in her stomach, though she was no longer hungry.

The tea should help to calm her down.

She put the kettle on and stood watching Ginger confronting the elf, from the safety of underneath the chair.

If Marcie hadn't been so frightened, she would've found the scene comical.

But somehow her ability to laugh right now had fled.

When the tea was ready, Marcie sat in the living room, listening to the weather report on the radio.

It wasn't until she finished her tea and took her cup back into the kitchen that she noticed a man wearing padded brown coveralls and a red knit ski mask outside, in front of her house, behind the loaner car.

Oh my God! Who is that man? And what is he doing here? Is he a burglar? Has he been inside this house, messing with that elf?

She moved to the sliding glass window, her phone in her hand ready to call 911, before she realized the man was Ted.

Ace was beside him now, barking and playing.

He held a shovel, which he'd used to shovel the snow behind the car.

"Oh my gosh," she said. "He didn't have to do that!"

Ginger stood at her side, looking out, wagging her tail. She barked once.

Marcie waved to him through the window, as he turned to look her way.

He waved back.

She held up a finger to tell him to wait a minute and then started pulling her coat and boots back on, bundling up to go back outside.

Once she was out the door, she hollered, "Hello."

"Hello," he said. "I thought you might be getting snowed in."

"I shoveled Ginger a path," Marcie spoke, as she grabbed her shovel, and trudged through the heavy snow toward him.

Once she reached him, their breath made clouds on the air, which puffed from their mouths and floated upward.

"It was really sweet of you to shovel for me, but you didn't have to do that," she said. "I was planning to come back out."

He shrugged. "I wanted to."

"Well, thank you," she said. "I'll have to bake you a pie, or some cookies, to repay you."

"No need to repay anything," he said.

But she'd seen the way his eyes lit up when she said cookies.

"I have everything to bake sugar Christmas cookies," she said. "So, I'll bring you some."

"Sounds delicious," he said.

She took her shovel and headed for the area from the house to the car.

The area behind the car had been shoveled, but not the area in front.

"What are you doing?" he asked.

"Shoveling the rest of the snow, and making a path to get to the car," she said.

"Go back inside, where it's warm," he said. "I'll finish the shoveling."

She hesitated, as he watched her.

She frowned slightly.

Not the reaction he'd expected.

Likely she wasn't used to anyone helping her.

He could change that.

"Tell you what. I could use a nice hot cup of coffee when I'm done. Black, no cream or sugar. Not decaffeinated."

"Oh. All right," she said. "I can do that. There's a coffee press inside."

"Even better," he said. "Go on inside. No point in us both getting cold."

Marcie nodded. "Okay."

Though she suddenly didn't feel like going back inside the house, where that creepy elf was, she headed back inside to fix his coffee.

As the snow fell softly, Zeke knew this night was perfect for the next part of his plan.

It would take him just two hours to drive from New York City to the Pocono Mountain house, and he would make good time before the roads got bad. The drive was a familiar one, and he wouldn't go slow.

He headed out and listened to heavy metal on the way to Beverly's place. She hated the music, but it brought out his strongest side, and he felt alive listening to it as he drove.

Once there, he found the usual perfect place to park and

made his way through the woods, following the path he normally took.

The cold had made the urge to urinate strong, so he stopped beside the tree where he usually stopped to relieve himself.

From the trees, he could see the darkened windows of the house.

Good. She's asleep.

He brushed the snow, making sure he left no footprints, no trace for anyone to see.

With soft snow it was easier. Nothing to sink down into, like a hard-packed snow would do, leaving a deep impression.

He felt like a kid at Christmas. Excited.

Moving the elf. Would it scare her?

She already didn't like the elf.

On the video, he'd heard her say she thought the elf was creepy.

That pleased him. He liked the idea of keeping her on edge. Building things slowly. Scaring her a little at first.

The house in the Poconos was easy to get into.

He'd made a key for himself. Anyone could have since naïve Beverly left her key under the mat.

She might act like a know-it-all at times and liked to get her way, but she knew nothing about her own safety and security.

That doormat was the first place a thief would look.

Zeke wasn't dating her for her brains, but for her connections, and to blend in with society people, as was expected of him.

He had family money and his career helped him fit in, but he knew he was a bit of an odd duck. With Beverly on his arm, people paid less attention to him, just the way he liked it.

Though Beverly was attractive, with huge breasts, they weren't real. She barely reacted when he squeezed them. He enjoyed her body only to a point, but she was so particular about what she would and would not do, that he needed another woman on the side, for his more unusual urges.

When he found a woman who fit his needs and desires, he kept her on the side, away from his society life.

If she lasted, she would take care of his other needs.

The kind polite society couldn't know about.

The kind that could land him in jail if anyone found out.

He'd make sure they never did.

He was always careful. That's why he never got caught.

Marcie would be his fourth woman on the side, and he felt confident that he'd gotten better at keeping a woman and easing her into what he demanded she do for him.

He wasn't going to think about the other three. They couldn't cause him trouble anymore, so there was no point in looking back or thinking about them now.

He was excited about the elf, and the camera.

Like a new toy, both were firsts for him and made the game more fun.

Moving through the house, in his stocking feet, after leaving his boots outside the door, he made sure Ginger didn't bark.

He'd studied the dog and ways to keep her quiet.

She hated the antique elf he'd bought Beverly, so he'd make sure she was in her kennel before he touched the elf, and he wouldn't let her see it.

Where is the elf? He paused, wondering.

It's somewhere dark because the camera only shows darkness unless it's photo time.

It's in that closet I'll bet. Where Marcie put it before.

The camera had showed him one time when she'd made

it face the kitchen wall. Then he could only see the wallpaper, which was no fun.

When she'd placed it somewhere dark, it was always dark, until photo time.

Being unable to watch her had made him decide to move the elf.

She'd hidden it away, so now he would take it back out.

Let her know the elf would not stay hidden. Let her think the elf was alive.

If she was even more scared of it, all the better.

Depending on how her mind worked, he could really mess with her.

Now he was inside the house, looking for the dog.

Ginger wouldn't bark at him.

Beverly and he had trained her not to, and he'd slipped in and out of the house in the dark several times when Beverly was sleeping.

This wouldn't be a change for the dog.

Patterns, everyone had patterns.

It was the key to taking the girls he collected.

It was the key to a lot of things.

He'd made a pattern, so that the dog would know his pattern and not react.

So far things were going perfectly.

Except for her hiding the elf.

Denying him the chance to see her.

Messing with her would be fun.

She'd been reacting to the elf, trying to exert her own control over the situation.

He could hear her sometimes, even when he couldn't see her.

He was determined to see her.

He liked watching women almost as much as touching

them. Especially when he could see the reactions in their eyes. Their fear was a huge turn on.

He could get excited just thinking about that, but he didn't have time for that now. He forced his thoughts away from the last stages of his plan and beyond. Tonight, he'd focus only on tonight.

Once the dog was enjoying her treat and he knew she would stay quiet, he found the elf quick enough on the top shelf of the coat closet.

There she is.

Hello there, Tananna. Wait till you and me get to watch Marcie later.

I have so many things planned.

And we'll have it all on tape for eternity, if this one doesn't last.

Taking the elf, without letting any of her bells jingle, he closed the closet door almost all the way, but left a gap.

Then he moved into the kitchen and placed the elf in the cabinet which held plates and bowls.

The bowls Marcie would use to make her breakfast oatmeal.

She was patterned with her oatmeal, so he knew she would make a bowl in the morning.

He wondered how long it would take her to notice the elf wasn't in the coat closet.

Would she get up for a snack later and look for it tonight?

Or would she find it in the kitchen cabinet in the morning?

How would she react to finding it beside her oatmeal bowl?

The temptation to creep upstairs and watch Marcie sleeping was strong, but he wouldn't.

Not yet.

He had to control his urges until he had her where he wanted her.

Luck was with him today, as the weather was cooperating. Large, white flakes of snow floated down to coat everything, which meant any footprints his boots left would be filled and any trace of him covered or eliminated.

It was supposed to fall heavily tonight and continue snowing for the next two days.

After leaving the elf in its new location, he gave Ginger another dog biscuit, part of his routine, whispered, "Good girl," and then slipped out of the house through the back door, locking it behind him.

He stepped back into his boots, after dumping the snow out of them, and put up with the cold damp of the inside of the boots.

A little discomfort was worth it.

He would turn the heat on in his car on the way back to the city to warm and dry his feet and socks again.

Brushing his tracks by the back door, just in case, he then moved through the woods to his car, which was parked in a different cove of the subdivision.

One where none of the owners were visiting this winter.

He had to make it back to his office in Manhattan as soon as possible.

Tonight, and early tomorrow, he had to do enough work that no one would suspect he hadn't been in the office working, late into the night.

It meant missing sleep, but he'd catch up when he flew back to Miami to be with Beverly.

She'd bitched when 'work' called him to leave, but understood work was important and that he made too much money to say no.

The flight back to Miami on a private charter wasn't much and the pilot was used to flying him with little notice.

Everything was going as planned.

Even if Marcie hid the elf again, she couldn't keep the elf hidden forever, because she had to take pictures of it every day.

Plans for his latest girl on the side were going to be fun.

Sometimes he had to be his own Santa Claus and come up with his own perfect gift.

This year he had picked Marcie.

MARCIE FIXED COFFEE FOR TED, while he finished shoveling, and then decided to put a few ginger snaps on a plate, since he seemed to like cookies.

They weren't the Christmas sugar cookies she'd promised to bake him, but they were what she had right now.

She liked keeping ginger snaps on hand because ginger was good for settling upset tummies. And her stomach was decidedly unhappy right now.

Marcie pulled the bag out of the pantry cabinet and set it on the counter.

The elf still lay on the floor, where she had thrown it.

She went into the downstairs bathroom and grabbed a bath towel to wrap around the elf, and then she ran back into the kitchen to cover that thing up, so she wouldn't have to look at it.

Wrapping the elf, she carried it back to the front closet and set it back on the top shelf.

"Stay," she hissed, before slamming the door.

If the thing were somehow alive, it would have heard her.

She had the urge to put something under the door, to keep it closed, but would wait until Ted went home.

She didn't want Ted to think she was crazy.

He was so nice, and she really liked him.

"I only have ginger snaps right now," she told him, as he entered the kitchen. "I'll just get us some plates."

"Cookies sound good." He went to the open cabinet which held the plates. Taking one down, he placed some cookies on it and carried it over to the table. "Have a cookie," he said.

"I'm supposed to be serving them to you," she said, realizing how distracted and upset the elf had made her.

How long had she been standing there, thinking about it?

"You can do that next time," he said. "Try one and let me know if they're any good."

She picked up a cookie and took a nibble.

"Yes, they are," she said.

"Good." Lifting his coffee cup, he sipped, and then pointed to the coffeepot. "Want some?"

"No," she shook her head. "I'm more a tea or hot cocoa drinker."

He smiled. "Point me to the hot cocoa."

She pointed; he went in that direction and found it.

Taking a cup, he filled it with water, and then put her mug in the microwave.

When it dinged, he took the cup out and mixed her hot cocoa, before carrying the mug over to her.

"Thank you for being so thoughtful," she said. "I didn't get to ask you what you do for a living the other day. We were so rushed at the grocery store."

"You're welcome," he said. "I'm in the Air Force. I fly jets."

"Oh," her eyes widened. "Wow. So, you're a fighter pilot."

"Yes," he nodded. "I'm based at Seymour Johnson Air Force Base, in North Carolina."

"What made you decide to be a fighter pilot?" She asked.

"I have a twin brother. Jack. I almost drowned when I was a kid and Jack saved me. He decided to go into the Marines and do search and rescue. I opted for the Air Force, because both the Navy and the Marines involve having to swim in extreme circumstances and I didn't want to do that."

"Wow," Marcie said.

"Mother and Dad say one son fights on the seas and the other fights in the air, so we've just about got everything covered."

Marcie laughed.

It was good to hear. He was glad to see the light in her eyes, which had seemed troubled before.

He wondered what had been troubling her.

"How long have you been in?" She asked.

"I was twenty-two, when I joined the Air Force, after college," he said. "Did two tours. Now that I'm in my thirties, I'm getting out."

"How long is a tour?"

"Usually four years," he said.

"What will you do after you get out?"

"Probably fly commercial planes."

"So, you will be flying people," she said.

"That's right." He nodded. "A bus driver in the sky."

"You make that sound rather unexciting," she said.

"I enjoy flying and I've already had plenty of exciting experiences." He smiled at her.

She couldn't help but smile back.

"Driving passengers isn't as exciting, but there will also be less danger."

"That's good," she said.

He changed the subject. "What about you? Have you always been a house-sitter?"

"Oh no." she shook her head. "Not always. My parents passed in a car accident while I was in my senior year of high school."

"Sorry to hear that," he said.

She nodded once and then went on. "After I graduated, I moved in with my boyfriend. I lived with him for four years, while he went through college, and we had planned to get married, right after he graduated. But when I got pregnant, he left me."

"He sounds like a selfish jerk."

"He was," she said. "Everything was always about him."

"So, you have a child." He stated, assuming she did.

Marcie shook her head. "No. Lost the baby the week after he left me."

"Oh no," he said. "I'm sorry for your loss."

She nodded again, and they both were silent for a moment.

He took her hand.

The moment his hand touched hers, it was as if a match had struck against a matchbox.

White heat flared between them.

They both felt the connection, the chemistry, as they gazed into each other's eyes.

She'd let down her guard by sharing very personal things about herself.

This connection was more than chemical.

The strength of it surprised him.

Blushing, she broke the connection first, pulling her hand away, looking far off, across his shoulder, not focusing on anything. "Thanks. It was a long time ago."

Her tone made it clear; she was done talking about it.

He changed the subject. "What made you consider house-sitting as a career?"

Something in her eyes shifted as she spoke, and he felt in his gut that she was going to share something deep about herself, not a typical answer.

"If I don't stay anywhere long, there's less chance I'll get attached," she said. "So, I live like a gypsy. I can be packed to be anywhere in the world in five minutes," she laughed, "and my passport is always ready."

"So can I." He smiled. "Travel can be good. Depending on the reason."

"And the season." She smiled back at him.

"And the season," he repeated. "What are you planning to do this Christmas Eve?"

"No plans really." She shrugged. "I'm used to being alone. It's just another day." She shrugged again.

It sounded like her defenses were up again. He wondered if they would come back down as they got to know each other.

She'd shared personal things quickly and that wasn't always best.

Good relationships took time.

"Well," he said. "It's all in how you look at it. I've spent holidays overseas, and I've missed traditional Christmases here."

He gave her another smile. "I believe that spending the holidays with someone who you care for is better than exchanging presents."

He watched her eyes light up.

Was that a glimmer in her eye that said she might be interested in spending Christmas with someone who cared?

He would wait until they'd gone on a few dates and then ask her if she'd like to spend Christmas with him.

They'd just met and they were getting to know each other, but he liked everything about her so far.

It would be fun to celebrate the holidays with her and Ginger.

Her mind seemed to have drifted again.

"What are you thinking?" he asked.

"That I have to take another stupid elf picture, today." She sighed.

"What elf picture?" He didn't know what she was talking about.

"The homeowner, Beverly, has this antique Christmas elf that she's entered in an online elf contest, and I have to take pictures of the stupid thing every day and text them to her."

"That doesn't sound so hard."

"No." She shrugged. "There's a list on the refrigerator that says what kind of pictures to take and when. She left a lot of instructions."

He got up and went over to read the list.

"Huh," he said. "That's a detailed list. Guess she is really into the whole elf contest thing."

"She sure is," Marcie said.

"So go take the picture," he said. "Get it over with."

"I was going to change the list around and do the elf with snow shovel one outside today since it snowed last night, and we've shoveled."

"Okay." He held out his hand. "Here. Give me your phone and I'll do it. Get the elf and let's get it over with. Then you can relax and have another cookie." He smiled at her.

His smile made her feel all melty.

If only it were so simple, she thought.

Relax and have another cookie. I need that on a T-shirt.

Him taking a picture would help, but that wouldn't answer her other concerns.

She wondered how to approach them.

"Do you think it would be hard for someone to break-in here?" she asked. "There are no neighbors close enough to see if a burglar was creeping around outside."

"It might be," he said. "Want me to check your doors and windows?"

"Yes," she said, a breath which she didn't know she'd been holding now releasing.

"I'll do that right now, and then go get the elf picture done." He stood and said, "I'll start with the basement, and work my way up to the second floor."

"Thanks," she said.

"I'll check all your locks. If you need new ones, I'll head to the hardware store."

"Okay. Though it's not my house," she said.

"But it is your safety," he said. "You can't stay alone in a building that won't lock properly. No matter whose building it is."

By the time he got done checking everything, she had the elf on the kitchen table, facing the wall again.

"Everything is secure," he said. "They're not getting in without a key or a lock pick."

"Oh, someone could still get in with those?" She frowned.

"Of course. You can't keep a professional thief out. Not without high-dollar systems and guards, but those guys are going after things like the crown jewels, not your middle-class jewelry boxes and electronics. And people don't leave valuables inside empty ski lodges in the Poconos."

"I understand," she said.

But if no one could get in, then how did that elf get moved?

I didn't imagine it moved. It was right beside the cereal bowl.

"I'll be right back," he said.

Taking her phone, he grabbed the elf off the table and went outside to take the picture with the snow shovel. On the way, he pulled his hat over his head and face.

After he came back in, he handed the phone to her and said, "I added my phone number, in case you need to call me. Anything scares you, night or day, you call. Okay?"

"Okay." She took the phone from him with a small smile. "I will."

"Good." He nodded. "Now I'll go see about your locks. Sit tight, I'll be back in a bit."

"Okay," she said.

After he walked away, she texted the elf photo to Beverly, along with a text message.

We had a lot of snow to shovel so I went ahead and did the elf shoveling snow pic while we have snow to shovel. Does anyone around here have a key to this house?

Beverly's reply was almost immediate.

You're supposed to be watching the Rudolph DVD, not shoveling snow. No, nobody has a key except you. Did you lose my key?

Marcie texted back. *No, I did not lose your key.*

Follow the instructions, Beverly texted. *If you expect a good reference.*

"This woman is unreal," Marcie muttered, as she put her phone in her pocket. "And I do not need her reference. I have plenty of good ones to use, if I need one."

CHAPTER 5

*B*everly had made Marcie mad, when she'd threatened to give her a bad reference. She didn't like the way the woman wanted to control everything she did.

She looked down at today's to-do list.

Day five: Take a picture of the elf on the desk with the phone, reporting to Santa.

"That is *not* happening," Marcie told Ginger. "Instead, we are going to go outside."

Happy barking was Ginger's response. She knew what outside meant.

Marcie hadn't watched the Rudolph DVD last night and she wasn't going to take the elf picture on the desk talking to Santa today, either.

Today she was going to build a snowman, because that would be fun, and the recently fallen snow was the very best kind of snow to build one.

She and Ginger also needed to get out of the house, into the fresh air.

Marcie bundled up, let Ginger out, and then they took a short walk, before coming back to play in the yard.

She tried throwing a rope toy for Ginger, but it would plop down into the snow, and then Ginger would run over to it and just poke it with her nose.

But she didn't like the cold snow on her muzzle, so she wasn't going to get in the cold snow to get a toy.

Instead, after she poked her nose at it, she turned to look at Marcie, wanting Marcie to get the toy for her.

Marcie laughed. "You're teaching me to play fetch, not the other way around."

"Woof," Ginger responded as her tail started wagging at something, or someone.

Marcie turned to look and saw Ted heading toward her.

"That dog is smart," Ted said.

"I didn't see or hear you coming," she said.

"That's because I'm stealthy," he said.

"Yes, you are."

She wasn't sure what she thought of that.

That could be a good thing, or a bad thing.

"I didn't fool Ginger, though," he said. "Good dog."

Ginger wagged her tail even more, and Ted bent down to scratch her ears.

"Have you had to be stealthy, in your life, much?" Marcie asked as she watched them.

"Not on the job, if that's what you mean," he said. "A plane can be stealthy, but I just fly the jets." He shrugged.

"Just fly them." She laughed. "The pilots I've met were not so modest. They were cockier, and tended to brag."

"Some are like that, yes," he said with a smile. "But not all."

Marcie smiled back at him. "I'm glad."

She was glad he was one of the nicer ones.

Some pilots are so full of themselves. I'm glad Ted isn't.

"So, when are you stealthy? If not on the job," she asked.

"You had to be stealthy if you wanted to nab any cookies before dinner," he said, giving her a wink.

She laughed. "I'll bet you and your brother got into mischief growing up."

"Some," he admitted.

She gave him a big smile. "Some." She shook her head. "I wonder what your mother would have to say about that."

"She'd tell you she knew we were sneaking cookies but didn't let on that she knew."

"Your mom sounds awesome."

"She is."

"I don't have any extended family still living and I was an only child," she said. "So, I'm alone in the world when it comes to relatives."

"I'm sorry to hear that," he said.

"I'm used to being alone during holidays." She shrugged. "I stay busy, and make my own celebrations. Today, I'm building a snowman."

"I'm used to family around the holidays, not to being alone," he said. "Though I always have Ace, it's not the same as human companionship. So, I'm glad we're both here this season. I'll help you build that snowman, if you'll let me."

"Sure," she said. "That would be great."

"Thanks," he said. "It will be fun."

They let the dogs loose to play and then began rolling the first big snowball, which would be the bottom of the snowman.

By the time they were done, they'd made a big round snowman.

Much bigger than Marcie would have made on her own.

"Whew," she said. "That was work. He looks great!"

"Yes, he does," Ted said.

Marcie had bought a big carrot for a snowman and had taken sticks from the kindling pile by the house to use for his arms.

A piece of red licorice for his mouth, two black stones for his eyes, and then he was finished.

"He needs a hat," Ted said. "I can bring over one of mine."

"That's great," Marcie said. "I only packed the one on my head and won't give it up."

"Yeah, don't do that. Keep your head warm. I've got this covered." Ted collected Ace and said, "Be back in just a few. Go inside and get warm."

"Okay. Want some hot cocoa? I'm making some," she said.

"Sure," he said. "Sounds good."

Marcie took Ginger and went inside where she stood in the kitchen, watching Ted go to his place.

He was a handsome man, much taller than her. Being around him made her feel safe and secure. He also knew how to make her smile and laugh.

Though she was used to being alone at Christmas, she was happy they were both here this season, too.

Maybe he will come over and celebrate Christmas with me. I'll wait till we know each other a little better and then I'll ask him.

The thought made her both excited and a little nervous.

She'd never asked a guy out before. This would be totally new.

Ted came back with a camouflage cap.

"Is that part of your uniform?" she asked.

She knew nothing about military men, or what each branch wore. She hadn't grown up around military bases, or had anyone in her family who'd served. And civilians often wore camo things.

"This is a USAF ABU hot weather cap," he said. "Standard issue. I don't have any uniforms here, but just happened to tuck this cap into my bag to leave here, if I ever need a good cap to wear in the summer."

"I don't think it gets very hot here," she said. "I always look a place up before I say yes to a job in a place I've never been. Looks like they get maybe two to three weeks of hot weather all summer."

"Yeah. Same. I bought this place to use as a ski house, and I can rent it out. I won't leave much personal stuff here; just basics. But these caps," he shrugged. "It's easy to get another."

"Well, it's perfect for our snowman," she said.

"Speaking of perfect, this snow is good for skiing," he said. "Have you thought about my invitation? Ready to go try Montage Mountain with me, this weekend?"

"I have, and I would like to, but I don't want you to be disappointed if I totally suck at it," she spoke, her soft voice getting lower with each word.

"Hey." He stepped closer and placed his finger beneath her chin, tilting her face up to look at him. "You won't disappoint me, and you're not going to suck at it."

She gave him a small smile. "Okay."

"We'll go tomorrow as planned, while the snow is good," he said. "Before we get a heavier snowfall."

"Okay. What time?"

"The dogs need to be walked in the morning. I'll come by with Ace, we'll walk them, and then we can head out right afterward."

"Sounds good. That way I'll get more time with Ace, so he can get more used to me."

"Right," he smiled. "Sounds like a plan. I'm looking forward to our date."

"Yes," she smiled back at him. "Me too."

She fixed them both a cup of hot cocoa, then took the elf out of the closet, and Ted went outside to take a picture of the elf with the snowman.

After he brought the elf back in, she got a picture of the elf with the cup of hot cocoa. "That's two more down and out of the way," she said.

When he left for his house, she texted the pictures to Beverly, along with a message.

Working ahead. Sending you one elf pic for today, and two elf pics for tomorrow.

Beverly's response wasn't a happy one.

YOU STUPID GIRL. DO YOU NOT KNOW HOW TO FOLLOW DIRECTIONS?

Marcie put her phone down to walk away, but then she turned back and picked up the phone again to text back.

There is no need to scream at me. And yes, I know how to follow directions.

Marcie was glad the woman was miles away.

"I hope I never have to meet her in person," she told Ginger, who wagged her tail.

THEN FOLLOW THEM! TAKE THE PICS IN ORDER LIKE I TOLD YOU!

Marcie put her phone down and stopped texting Beverly back and reading her texts.

She knew there was no point trying to have a conversation with an angry, crazy person.

Wow. Just wow. Beverly has issues.

We would rub each other the wrong way if we were in the

same room. It's a good thing we aren't, and it's best to keep it that way.

Beverly gave no reason why she wanted Marcie to take the pictures in the order she'd laid out on the list.

And how could I have taken the elf shoveling the snow pictures if there wasn't any snow to shovel?

Each change Marcie made had a reason for the change, and a logic that Marcie understood.

She would have explained had Beverly been a more reasonable person.

But she was not reasonable at all.

Marcie had never house-sat, or pet-sat, for a client who screamed at her over text messages.

For the first time, she was seriously considering firing a client.

But then Ginger hopped up next to her on the couch and tried to give her kisses.

Laughing, because it tickled and the little dog was so adorable, Marcie said, "You can tell I'm upset, can't you, you dear sweet little dog."

She picked Ginger up and snuggled with her, enjoying the little kisses and the softness of her fur.

She couldn't quit on this sweet little dog.

If she had to put up with text screaming, at least she could put the phone down or even turn it off. She didn't have to answer it.

Beverly wasn't likely to fire Marcie.

Then who would she get to take care of her little dog and do the stupid elf contest things required?

But one thing was for sure.

Marcie would never work for her again, nor would she ever use her for a reference.

The woman was unbalanced and had no control over

her temper.

~

*Day six: Elf makes hot cocoa and shares it with you. Then show
him climbing the tree because he had too much sugar.*

MARCIE WASN'T TAKING any elf pictures today, because today
she had a ski date with Ted.

He'd come over with Ace earlier and they'd walked both
dogs, and now Marcie and Ted were in his car heading to
Montage Mountain in Scranton, Pennsylvania.

She'd never been to a ski resort before, but last night
she'd looked up Montage Mountain Ski Resort and Water-
park on the internet. Though the website had explained a
lot to her already, she was still full of questions.

She took a deep breath and started in. "So, I went on the
website for the resort, and it said there are single and double
black diamonds, and blue diamonds, and green diamonds.
Is that what they are calling the mountains?"

"That's how they rank the trails, according to difficulty,"
Ted explained. "It starts with green diamond, then blue
diamond, and then finally black diamond which is the
hardest of all. That would be an expert-level trail. You'll only
be skiing on green diamond trails today, after you have a
lesson on how to ski on the bunny trail."

"Oh, they call it a bunny trail? That must make me a
ski bunny." She laughed. "Okay. Which trails do you
ski on?"

"I can ski on any of them," he said.

"Even the big black diamond ones? I read on the
internet that there's one thousand vertical feet and one trail
is called white lightning."

"I can ski any trail, anywhere. Learned to snow ski when I was twelve."

"Wow. So young."

"Our uncle loved to ski. We went once a year, with him and his kids, to a ski lodge and had a family week."

"Wow. So, do you have a big extended family?" He'd already told her about his brother and their parents.

"There's my twin brother, Jack, our parents, one uncle, his wife, and their three kids. Not a real big family, just average."

"That's a lot more than I have."

He reached his hand across to cover hers and squeezed. "That must be hard, especially during the holidays. Where would home be for you if you went back anywhere?"

"I don't really have roots anywhere," she said. "Just a small storage unit in my hometown in Ohio. When I'm not house-sitting, I stay in extended-stay hotels or at a friend's house, since it's never very long that I'm not working. I've been able to travel to some very cool places, though."

"I've been all over, too," he said. "But I decided to start putting some roots down. This is my first house. I'll wait a few years till I know where I want to live year-round and then I'll buy a second home."

"Sounds like a good plan," she said.

"So, before we get there, you've got a couple choices today, Marcie. I can sign you up for the beginner class and then we'll ski, or I can teach you."

She watched his face to see which of the two choices he might prefer, but seeing that there seemed to be no difference, she said, "Maybe the beginner class? Then I'd be with other beginners and not feel stupid."

He gave her a quick glance. "You're far from stupid. And

there's nothing stupid about being a beginner. Everyone is a beginner, at first."

"Yeah, I guess you're right," she said.

"You're an intelligent woman who just hasn't learned a particular skill yet," he said.

"That's a nice way to put it." She smiled at him.

"Nothing but the truth," he said.

"So, after the beginner class I'll go on the bigger trail."

She was not feeling confident, and it showed in her voice.

"Yes.," he said." The bunny slope will have a gradual decline, so you can get used to it and your new skills. Then we'll go down one of the easy green diamond slopes. Don't worry, I won't take you on anything too hard for a beginner, or too scary."

"Okay," she said.

So far, Ted had been nothing but kind and thoughtful, and now, on their first date, he was looking out for her and taking care of everything.

She really liked him ... a lot.

When they arrived at Montage Mountain, they got out, and went inside the lodge, to look for the ski rental place, and to sign Marcie up for a beginner class.

She would take the two-hour beginner class, then they'd ride the shuttle lift to the top of the mountain and then ski down together.

Marcie would ski down a mountain for the first time in her life, and she did not feel ready.

Her nervousness had kicked in, along with a few insecurities.

What if I'm a lousy skier? What if I get hurt?

This was the most unique first date Marcie had ever been on.

First dates usually made her nervous, but not to this degree.

This time she had the added nervousness of learning to ski.

She couldn't believe she was going to learn how to ski, with a handsome Air Force pilot.

Mr. TDH was also hot and kind. Everything a girl might wish for in one guy.

If she hadn't been sitting right next to him in the car, she might have pinched herself.

After spending time with him, he felt less like "Mr. TDH" and more like just handsome and kind Ted.

"I'll stay and watch you for a short while," he said. "And then, I'll take a run down one of the other, more advanced trails. But I'll be back before your class is over."

"Okay," she said.

When she got nervous, she wasn't as talkative.

After purchasing lift tickets, and a class for Marcie, they headed for the ski rental counter.

Ted rented the equipment, ski boots, poles, and skis and then helped her put her boots on.

The boots felt heavy and clumsy on her feet before she ever stepped onto the skis.

She awkwardly walked with him to the bunny hill.

Marcie eyed the bunny slope with trepidation.

A few feet away from it, he helped her step onto her skis and made sure her heavy boots were attached correctly.

Then she had to move closer to the bunny hill.

Thank God for these poles, or I don't know how I would've moved. This is much harder than it looks.

Soon she was on the bunny slope, in the class, listening to her instructor.

Then it was her turn to ski on the bunny slope, with the other beginners.

She slowly made the moves, copying what her instructor had showed them, trying not to mess up.

Ted waited for Marcie patiently, while she took the beginner class, until he saw she was starting to get the hang of it.

She'd learned how to snowplow to stop, which was the first thing to learn, and one of the most important things.

He went off to take a run down one of the bigger diamonds.

She watched him head off, before redirecting her attention to her instructor.

Soon the class was over, and Ted was back waiting for her to finish.

"You're doing great!" Ted said. "All set? Ready to ride up to the top with me?"

"I think so," Marcie said. "Ready as I'll ever be."

He held out his gloved hand for her, and she placed her gloved hand in his.

Then he gave her hand a squeeze, and they took up their poles and headed for the shuttle lift, which would take them to the top of the mountain.

Marcie watched the lift seats came around, almost popping people on the butt or legs.

She watched how people sat down in them before the seats ran into the backs of their legs and then kept going up the mountain.

Eyeing the one they would be on, now that their turn had come, she hoped the seat would be easy to sit down on.

She hoped she wouldn't fall and embarrass herself, and him.

But then, the seat was behind them, coming fast, and as it touched the backs of her legs, she sat, fast, along with Ted.

She laughed.

That hadn't been so bad. Maybe the actual skiing will be okay too and I won't crash or break anything.

He put his arm across the back of the ski lift seat and smiled down at her. "Nervous?" he asked, his voice kind.

"A little," she said. Though in truth, she was nervous a *lot*, not a little.

"You'll do just fine," he said.

She hoped he was right. She didn't want to look foolish on the bigger hill, among all the experienced skiers, and she didn't want to do anything that would ruin their first date.

How can he be so relaxed? Don't first dates make him nervous?

If so, he certainly isn't showing it. Confidence is in every move he makes, and in everything he says and does.

If she could make it down this hill, and not make a fool of herself, then this first date would be a success.

And then, maybe they'd have another one.

She wondered what it would feel like to kiss him. And if he would try to kiss her. She hoped he liked her at least half as much as she liked him.

"I hope so," she answered him; her current thoughts more on kissing him than on skiing.

That was probably a good thing. His nearness was sending her senses into overdrive.

His arm reached around her shoulders, pulling her closer.

He smelled so good.

"You'll be fine, and I'm right here, if you need me."

"Thank you," she said, breathing in his masculine scent

and warming up beneath the bundle of clothes she was wearing.

When they reached the top of the hill, where they needed to get off of the lift, Marcie did everything the instructor had told her to do, but there was a patch of ice beneath her skis, which no one had mentioned, and her feet shot out from under her, knocking her flat on her butt onto the hard ice.

With her legs bent and her feet still in the skis, she slid fast.

She screamed, as she went sliding the mountain faster than she wanted, on her butt, and now leaning backward, her skis doing nothing to stop her.

Snowplow! Snowplow!

How do you do that on your butt? I don't know how to stop like this! Or how to even get up!

Everything she'd learned had been from a standing position.

She had no idea what to do.

Her heart was racing.

Then Ted was there, next to her, forcing his skis against hers, making her stop.

She sat in the snow, red-faced, overheated, full of adrenaline, and with her heart pounding so fast she felt it in her ears.

Her fear rapidly turned to embarrassment.

So many people are watching.

She hung her head.

"Hey, babe," he said, his voice low and comforting. "You did fine. You just weren't ready to hit a patch of ice. It's okay. Ice respects no one, not even expert skiers. Come on, now. Let's get you up and try again."

Mortified, and wanting nothing more than to sit in the

lodge with a cup of their hot mulled wine, she took the hand he held out to her and let him help her up.

She'd have had no idea how to get herself up off the ground from her position if he hadn't helped her.

"I may not be so good at this," she said.

"Don't give up on it, yet," he said. "You haven't really had a chance to try. Without the ice, you would've been fine." He gave her an encouraging smile. "Come on, let's try it again, down the rest of the hill. Together."

"Okay," she said. But her face still burned, and she didn't know if she'd ever get over the embarrassment. And now her butt was cold, and she just wanted to get warm ... in the lodge ... with a hot drink.

Or back at the house, where she could cuddle with Ginger.

They skied down the rest of the hill, and it went okay.

Then they tried another trail, which had no ice beneath the shuttle lift drop off.

"You did great," Ted said.

She was a beginner and, in her mind, felt she wasn't good at this ... at all. "I guess. For a beginner," she said.

With Ted's encouragement, she kept trying and soon they were done skiing for the day.

"Come on," he said. "Let's go inside and get you warmed up. How does a mug of hot mulled wine sound?"

"I've never had it before, but it sounds really good," she said.

They sat together in the lodge, drinking hot mulled wine, as they watched the other skiers through the big window.

Marcie swore this was the best hot drink she'd ever had.

Then they drove back toward Gouldsboro, Pennsylvania, the quiet little town on top of a mountain in the Poconos.

Marcie was getting a real taste of ski country and all it entailed.

The drive was quiet, as Marcie was tired, and Ted had turned on music they both liked.

Every so often, he would reach for her hand, give it a squeeze, and she would smile at him.

Then she was 'home,' or at least home for her for the rest of the month before she moved on.

They didn't talk about that, although they both knew that was what she would do.

After he parked, he came around to her door and opened it to help her out.

She liked his chivalrous manners and his kindness.

For the first time, since she had begun house-sitting, she wished she wouldn't be moving on to another house-sitting job so soon.

He walked her to the front door and, as they turned to each other, he cupped her cheeks in his hands and pulled her close as he bent to kiss her.

Her eyes closed and as his lips met hers, she breathed in sharply at the intensity of their lips meeting and the way he tasted and felt.

It was the kind of kiss you would remember for a lifetime. The kind that felt so good physically, it went beyond the physical and deep into the soul.

She could have stayed there forever, but he let them come up for air.

"Wow," he said.

Her eyes, widened, looking deep into his, and seeing a similar response from him, she whispered, "Yes. Wow."

"It doesn't get better than this, sweet," he said. "I'll see you in before I go, but I have to say, I want to do this again."

"The skiing?" she asked.

He leaned in, his lips near her ear, and then whispered, "The kissing."

Tingles from his words and the touch of his lips on her ear sent goosebumps down her neck and back.

"Yes," she whispered back. "I want to do that again, too."

He pulled back and smiled at her. "So, a second date is on?"

"Oh, yes," she said. "Most definitely."

"Good," he said. "We could go skiing again, if you want, or we could do something else."

"Let's do something warmer," she said.

"Good," he said. "Got your key?"

"Hmm?" she frowned. "Oh yeah, my key."

She bent down and began fumbling beneath the front doormat, as he watched.

"What are you doing?" he asked. "Don't tell me that's where you keep the house key."

"Yes, well." Her face turned red as she looked up at him, now with the key in her hand. "It is."

"There's no point locking your door, if you're going to keep a key there," he said sternly. "That's the first place anyone would look."

"I have to keep it there for the cleaning lady," she explained. "Beverly's instructions."

"Nope," he said. "Not happening. Not with my girl. Let me see your keyring."

Marcie pulled out her keyring and handed it to him.

Deep down, she was happy he was making this decision for her, to keep her safe.

She hadn't felt right about that key under the mat since day one and should never have agreed to it.

No wonder the elf got moved. Someone got hold of this key, because I left it under there, and they are messing with me. How stupid of me to leave the key there for them.

Part of her wanted to talk to Ted about the elf being moved, and part of her did not.

She didn't know him that well yet and didn't want to drive him away. He might think she was crazy.

It would look crazy to someone else, but she knew that elf had moved.

But who had moved it?

The why was much easier.

Someone wanted to scare her.

CHAPTER 6

After putting the key on Marcie's keyring for her, Ted took the key and unlocked and opened the door.

"Stay behind me," he said. "I want to check the place out."

"Okay," she said.

He walked through the tri-level house, making sure it was safe, with no intruders. "All clear," he said.

"Do you always do that?" she asked.

"With my lady, yes," he said. "I need to make sure you're safe."

She liked that. Liked it a whole lot. Being 'his lady,' and being looked after like this.

No one had looked after her since she was a teenager, and she had forgotten how nice it felt to be cared for that way.

It felt so good not to be the one having to check all the doors and windows, just so she could sleep at night.

And it felt good to know she could call him if she needed him.

He came to where she stood, just inside the front door, with a happy smile on her lips. His gaze dropped to her lips.

Then he was pulling her close again, his lips descending on hers, and as their lips met again, she softly parted hers.

His tongue, slid in, teasing, testing, touching, as she melted like a snowball in the sun. Slow, warm, and melty.

That was how he left her, as he pulled away, saying, "One time was not enough."

"Mm-hmm," she murmured, her lips still feeling the aftereffects of his, and not wanting that feeling to go away.

"Goodnight, sweet Marcie," he said.

"Goodnight," she replied.

"Remember to lock the door behind me."

She nodded. "I will."

****

Marcie was warm and snug in bed, sleeping, when incoming texts at 2 a.m. woke her.

YOU DIDN'T FINISH THE ELF PICS. WHERE IS MY ELF IN THE TREE PIC?

The message repeated multiple times, as Beverly blew up Marcie's phone.

"Ugh, that stupid elf and those pictures," Marcie grumbled to herself, as she sat up in bed.

There would be no sleep once those texts started.

Marcie made herself crawl out of bed, not bothering to pull on a robe or her nightgown.

Wearing only her white lace panties, she stumbled downstairs, grabbed the elf from the closet ,and hurried about the room, wishing she owned warm pajamas to sleep in.

She'd been so tired the night before that she'd not taken the time to do anything but strip down to her underwear.

The big blankets were plenty warm she'd told herself.

Marcie posed the elf in the tree and then took a picture of it.

She texted back with the picture.

Sorry. Forgot about the tree part. You have the hot cocoa one already.

A long ranting text came back, but she didn't bother to read it.

Taking the elf out of the tree, her phone dinged again, but she ignored it.

Realizing she was thirsty; she went into the kitchen still holding her phone and the elf and then and sat them on the kitchen table, so she could and pour herself a glass of water.

She drank it down and then refilled it to carry it back upstairs. She didn't even look at her phone again.

It could stay down here where it wouldn't wake her again tonight. The phone wasn't turned off, but it was now on silent, and text messages wouldn't wake her all the way upstairs.

Trudging up the stairs, she shivered, looking forward to the warm bed again.

She was too tired to realize she'd left the elf out on the kitchen counter, where it would greet her in the morning.

THE CAMERA inside the elf's eye recorded the footage from where she'd sat the elf on the kitchen table, as she got herself some water.

Yeah, now that's more like it, my little elf's helper. Watch those titties bounce. And those white lace panties, those are nice. I knew you were a good girl, not the slutty kind. Sweet and inno-cent, that's my girl. I have so much to teach you.

He watched the footage over and over.

She moved about the kitchen, obviously put out, about having to do all this to take a picture of the elf.

But that was good, as it made her breasts bounce more.

He collected the footage, copied it, and added it to his collection of photos of her, then a few made prints and hung them up on his wall.

So far, he had pictures of her lips, breasts, and face. Soon he would add more.

He went over his plan in his head again.

Not long now, my girl. Then I'll be able to touch those round breasts and all your other goodies. Touch and take. To use when-ever and however I please. For as long as I please. As often as I please.

Who would miss you? No family. All alone at Christmas. Poor baby.

But don't worry. You won't be alone for long. Soon, it will be just me and you.

This summer he'd soundproofed the cabin. He'd moved the big iron bed downstairs, and attached arm and leg restraints to it.

There were jugs of water lined up along the kitchen wall, and the refrigerator and freezer were stocked.

A few weeks ago, he'd even ordered a red baby doll nightie, just for her. Red see-through material and white fur; it was the perfect outfit for an elf's helper.

He couldn't wait to see her in it and to watch those titties through the see-through material.

He rewound the video to watch her bare breasts again.

He'd never get tired of watching them.

~

Day seven: Watch a Christmas DVD with the elf, in the living room.

THE LIST of days had been jumbled around, after Marcie deviated from the order of things.

Today she was supposed to watch the Rudolph DVD with the elf, while munching on popcorn.

That would have been okay, before Ted asked Marcie out on another date.

So tonight, instead of the movie, Ted would take Marcie to an Italian restaurant in Scranton, which was an hour away.

Marcie would have to fake the elf photo later tonight, before she went to bed, and not really watch the movie or eat the popcorn.

But if she did that, she couldn't forget to send it.

She wouldn't waste the popcorn; she could always put the popcorn out for the birds.

Or she could do a different elf picture today instead and have Ted over to watch the movie with her.

That might be more fun.

Ted would be here any minute, and Marcie still didn't have her makeup done. She leaned closer to the mirror to put mascara on the other eyelash and tried not to blink.

She was wearing her favorite winter dress, green velvet with long sleeves and a scoop neck.

She didn't know why she'd packed the dress at the last minute. Ordinarily, she wouldn't have had anywhere to wear it, but she loved the soft velvet dress and had thought she could have a festive dinner at home for one, instead of two, since she wasn't seeing anybody and would be alone for the holiday.

Ted arrived, just as Marcie finished putting her lipstick on.

She hurried down the stairs to let him in. She opened the door, slightly out of breath.

He took one look at her and said, "Wow."

A huge smile spread across her face. "Thank you."

She looked down at her dress, still smiling. "This is my favorite dress."

"You look stunning in that dress," he said.

Heat filled her face and chest, and she knew the reddish blush had spread across her pale skin, which would now be slightly warm to the touch.

His gaze took this in, his eyes tender and appreciative.

The soulful expression in his eyes spoke to something deep within her, that she had no words for.

It was there again, that soul kind of gazing, the kind that needed no words.

"Are you ready?" he asked.

"Yes," she said. "I am."

She'd already seen to Ginger, who was in her crate for the evening, pouting.

The little dog was used to Marcie's constant presence.

But a woman had to go out occasionally, on a date or with friends.

Ted helped her on with her coat, then she grabbed her purse, and they were out the door.

"Where are we headed?" she asked. "I mean, I know we're going to an Italian place down in Scranton, but what's the name of it?"

"Sidel's Restaurant," he said. "I asked my realtor to

suggest a few good places, and this was the one she said had good, homemade-style Italian food."

"Oh, good," she said.

"Scranton has an interesting history," he said, as he opened the door for her.

She got in and he closed the door.

After he came around to the driver's side, got in, and started the car, he said, "Would you like to hear what I've learned about the city?"

"Oh yes, I would," she said. "I love history."

He backed the car out and headed onto the street.

"Me too," he said, as he smiled at her.

Turning back to watching the road, he said, "Scranton was a coal mining town. Many different ethnic groups came to work the mines and they settled into sections. The Italians in one area, the Irish in another, then the Polish, and the Welsh. You get the idea."

"Yes," she nodded.

"The groups liked to keep to themselves. They lived together, in sections. So, there would be the Italian section, the Welsh section, etc. Which isn't all that unusual for immigrants."

"Right. Because they spoke the same language," she said. "It just makes sense."

"Yes. But it gets even more interesting. For instance, the Irish Catholics, and the Italian Catholics, might have each had a church, one on one side of the street and the other on the other side. But they wouldn't cross the sidewalk in front of the other church. Even today, someone's grandmother might cross the street, so she doesn't have to walk in front of the other church."

"Wow, that seems a little crazy," she said.

"To us today, it does. But that's just how it was back

then," he said. "Also, with the different areas, because they were keeping alive things from the 'old country,' the food is very authentic, and recipes were handed down through the families. As a result, you will find good, authentic, ethnic foods of many types in Scranton, Pennsylvania."

"How cool," she said. "I'm glad you found an Italian place for us. I love Italian food."

"Me too," Ted said.

After the hour-long drive to the restaurant, they were both hungry.

Finally, they arrived and were seated inside. The waiter handed them each a menu.

"Order anything you want," Ted said. "Their specialty pasta sounds good."

"It does," Marcie said. "Large scallops on a bed of linguini in a sherry cream sauce sounds heavenly. I might order that."

Their waiter came to take their order, and they both ordered the house special, with side salads and glasses of wine.

Marcie wasn't much of a drinker, and she would have been worried about the hour-long drive back home, after Ted had been drinking, but Ted eased her worry immediately, when he said he wasn't interested in ordering a bottle of wine.

"I don't drink often and only have one glass when I do," she said. "It goes right to my head, real fast."

"I'll have to remember that," he said.

"Oh, so you can take advantage of me?" she asked.

"Sweetheart,' he shook his head. "I would never take advantage of you," he said. "You'll decide with your clear-headed free will, or nothing will happen."

"Oh, good," she said. "I try not to make any decisions if

I've had anything to drink. Mostly, I just get sleepy. It used to drive my girlfriends crazy. They'd be ready to party and there was sleepy Marcie over in the corner, dozing off, because she'd had a little too much wine."

He laughed. "Not the life of the party, then."

"Far from it." She laughed with him. "If you want me perky, do not give me alcohol."

"Noted," he said.

Their salads arrived, and he waited for her to take a bite of hers. "Good?"

She took a bite, nodded, and smiled.

"All right," he said, before digging in.

The waiter came with fresh bread, and fresh grated parmesan cheese for their salads.

"Thank you," Ted said, before the waiter left their table.

Marcie liked that he was nice to the staff.

You could tell a lot about a person by how they treated the waitstaff. She'd learned that lesson the hard way, with a few men who weren't so nice to the waiters.

When the main course came, Marcie's eyes widened.

The five scallops, mixed in with the pasta on each of their plates, were huge.

"One of these is enough for two," Marcie said. "I'll never be able to eat it all."

"Then you can take it home," he said. "And have it for lunch or for dinner tomorrow."

They let the waiter grate fresh parmesan cheese on top of each of their dishes.

It was the perfect topping.

By the time they'd eaten their fill, neither had room for dessert.

Ted asked for the check and a couple of to-go boxes.

Soon they were on their way home.

Marcie was full, a little tipsy, and sleepy. In the car, she leaned her head back against the headrest and enjoyed the heater, which blew warm air on her feet and legs. She'd forgotten how cold it could be wearing a dress, hose, and heels.

But she liked dressing up and she liked having somewhere nice to go when she was all dressed up. It had been a long time since she'd done that.

"If you're sleepy, go ahead and close your eyes," Ted said. "We've got an hour drive; I'll wake you when we get there."

Though it was nice of him to offer, she wasn't about to fall asleep on their second date.

She wanted to spend as much time around him as possible, especially as she'd be leaving at the end of the month and might never see him again.

That thought made her heart sad.

Now where had that sadness come from?

They hadn't known each other long.

She was used to leaving, moving on to the next job, and had never felt a reluctance to move on before. Never felt like she wanted to stay around a place, or a person, after the job was done.

What is so different about him?

She didn't know.

But he was.

And she was feeling different, this time.

She wanted to be around him more. As much as she could.

Riding in the car with him had felt like the place she was meant to be.

Every time she was around him, she had that feeling. It wasn't a thing she could have explained to anyone.

It just was.

He feels like home. But I need to stop thinking about that.

She had to change the subject and get her mind off that track. "Do you know what Beverly wanted me to do with that elf tonight?"

"I don't remember," he said. "Let me guess. She wanted you to build a Christmas village out of peppermint sticks, chocolate bars, and tinsel with the elf, while wearing a Grecian gown and reciting Ode to my Biggest Best Pain in the Ass Elf?"

Marcie laughed so hard; her stomach hurt. "No, no, that's not it," she gasped, "but that is funny. Oh, don't give her that idea." She laughed again. "Because that would surely be next!"

"Don't worry," he said. "I won't. Now, tell me what she wanted you to do today and what you sent her."

"I haven't sent her anything yet," Marcie said. "Because I haven't done anything. I switched the days, so I could get the shoveling one in and the hot cocoa ones in. The next ones are a little more involved. Tonight was supposed to be watching the Rudolph movie and eating popcorn, and tomorrow is baking Christmas cookies."

"Do the cookie one," he said. "And save me some."

"I'd already planned to do the cookie one tomorrow," she said. "Do you want to come over for cookies?"

He sent her a look that said: Really? You must know I want to come over and eat cookies. "Uh, yes. And you should know, I will *always* want to eat your cookies." He waggled his eyebrows at her.

She giggled.

He'd made it sound like it was more than cookies that he wanted to eat, and she was not normally dirty minded.

"I'm glad you want to eat my cookies," she said, still giggling.

"Mm, can't wait," was his reply.

She leaned back in the seat again, smiling, and dozed off before they reached her house.

"We're here, sweetheart," he spoke softly, waking her. "Home again, home again."

From wherever she was, in a dream, she heard his voice and woke.

"Hmm? Are we there already?"

"We are there," he said.

"I'm sorry I fell asleep."

"Don't be sorry. I don't mind."

"Well, it's our second date and it seems kind of rude to be falling asleep when we drive home after."

He put his finger under her chin. "You do not have a rude bone in your body. You told me drinking makes you sleepy. I gave you wine and you dozed off. No surprise because you were honest. This was a good second date. I'm glad you feel relaxed enough with me to fall asleep. Now stop worrying and relax."

She smiled, and then he leaned over and kissed her.

This kiss, like the two kisses from their first date, was a kiss for a lifetime memory, but was more relaxed because they'd kissed before and everything was less new.

Their tongues met and began a slow tasting, touching.

A dance.

One which would steam up the car, heat up their bodies, and leave them each longing for more.

When they came up for air, he said, "I need to get you into the warm house."

"It won't be as warm as you think," she said. "The fireplace hasn't had logs added to it, to keep it warm and toasty."

"I can remedy that," he said.

"Okay," she said. "I was going to ask you about where to get more firewood and forgot all about it tonight."

His face and tone turned serious. "I'll check your woodpile, and if you need more wood, I'll bring you some of mine."

"Thank you," she said. "I wasn't sure what to do. I'm a city girl. I don't even know how to chop wood."

"You don't need to chop wood," he said. "I'll take care of it for you."

She realized then that he'd been looking out for her, since she'd met him, in one way or another.

Normally, she was a little more independent.

But, because it was him, she really liked it.

"I appreciate the way you look out for me," she said. "It's very nice."

He bent to kiss her again.

Their lips touched briefly, in the softest, sweetest kiss.

"My pleasure," he said.

A text from Beverly interrupted the tender moment before it could go any further.

Where is my photo for today? We won't win if you don't do your job. You failed last night. And now you're doing it again. Call me.

Ted saw the text, as she read it to herself.

When she looked back up at him, he said, "Don't call her tonight. It's late. It's Saturday night. If you have to call her, call her tomorrow."

"Yeah, you're right. I'm not calling her tonight. She acts like I don't have a life, other than to jump and do everything she tells me to. Which she is not paying extra for. And she yelled at me via text the other night. If I don't do the picture she wants, on the day she wants, she loses it."

"I thought she was on vacation with her boyfriend?" Ted

raised an eyebrow. "Where is he? Seems like she ought to be busy with him."

"Yeah, I don't know. She messages me back right after I text her a picture, so she must live on her cell phone twenty-four/seven. This job is the weirdest one I've ever had. And I hate that old elf. It's creepy."

"I agree with you," he said. "They could make a Hollywood movie out of that one. A creepy doll story."

"I swear I think its eyes follow me," Marcie said. "But when I double-check, the eyes are staying still. And I know doll eyes can't follow me."

"No, they can't" he said. "Now, about those cookies..."

""You want to help me bake them?" she asked.

"I want to watch you bake them and lick the batter," he said. "I want to lick everything."

"Everything?" her voice squeaked.

His voice lowered. "Everything."

There was no question that he meant more than licking the bowl, the beaters, and the spatula.

"I would like that too," she said, feeling the heat rise up her neck.

"Yes," he said. "I guarantee you will."

Day eight: Elf in the kitchen baking Christmas cookies.
The sugar cut-out kind. The supplies are in the kitchen already. I want the kind you make from scratch, not the kind you slice and bake. No store-bought ready-made! There needs to be flour on the table and show the elf with the rolling pin.

Marcie read today's scheduled task from the list which she'd pinned on the refrigerator door with a magnet and shook her head.

"What a bossy woman your owner is," she said to Ginger.

Ginger barked back, as if agreeing.

Marcie was happy today, after the great date she'd had with Ted last night and the fact she was now making these cookies, more for Ted than the contest.

As much as he liked cookies, she hoped he liked hers.

And she suspected they would both be doing more than baking, and enjoying cookies, later this afternoon.

Marcie opened the refrigerator door and got two tubes of slice-and-bake sugar cookies out. "Cookies, check."

She placed them on the table and then went to the cupboard, where the flour was stored.

Ginger followed her over and stood wagging her tail.

"I can put flour on the table with the rolling pin and the dough rolled out and no one will be able to tell, by the pictures, whether I mixed the dough myself," Marcie said.

Ginger barked twice and followed her to the table, where Marcie set the flour canister down.

"We won't tell, will we, girl?"

Ginger barked once.

"Now I just need the wax paper and the rolling pin so I can set the scene," Marcie looked down at the little dog, "Once it's set, I'll have to go get that elf."

Ginger's bark changed at the mention of that elf. She did not like the elf ... at all.

Marcie put the wax paper on the table and then sprinkled some flour across it before placing the sugar cookie dough on it.

Then she took the rolling pin and rolled the dough out.

Taking a bell-shaped cookie cutter, she cut one cookie out.

Then using a star-shaped cutter, she cut another.

She continued until there were six of each and sprinkled more flour around.

Ginger had been quietly standing by her side, wagging her tail, likely hoping Marcie would drop some food on the floor, or hold it out in her hand.

"I've got to wash my hands before I go get that antique elf," she said. "Beverly would have a fit if I got anything on that elf."

Ginger stopped wagging her tail and loudly barked three times.

"Yes, I know you don't like her," Marcie said. "But I do need the other half of my pay, so let's not make Beverly mad."

She walked to the sink and turned the water on, ran her hands under the water, and then reached for the soap.

Ginger plunked down on the rug in front of the counter with what sounded to Marcie like a doggie humph.

She laughed and said, "This won't take long. And I'll put the elf away somewhere after we're done with today's picture. I didn't mean to leave her in the kitchen the other night. Sorry about that."

Ginger just gave her an exasperated look from her place on the rug.

Marcie went to get the elf, took the picture, and then put the elf back. "See," she said to Ginger, "all better now. No more elf today. And Ted is coming over. Later tonight, after we have cookies, he's going to watch Rudolph with us."

Ginger stood and started wagging her tail.

Woof.

"You like Ted, don't you, girl?"

Ginger barked again.

"I thought you did. I like him, too." Marcie smiled. "I like him a lot. Now, let's hope he likes my cookies as much as he says he will."

Then Ted was there, knocking on the door, and she went to let him in.

"Come on in," she said. "I'm just getting ready to put the first batch of cookies in the oven. I've already taken the elf picture and put that thing away in the closet."

She gestured to the coat closet.

He stepped inside and took off his coat and hat.

"I'll let you put them away, since I have flour all over me," she laughed. "Wouldn't want to get it on your coat."

"You sure do." He touched the tip of her nose. "Flour here." Then he bent to brush her lips softly with his in a gentle kiss. "And here."

She laughed, but wished he'd kiss her again, just like that. She couldn't get enough.

He pointed to the closet. "Ginger still barking at the elf every time you take it out?"

"Yes," she said. "Every time."

True to her word, the little dog came up to Ted to say hello, but then barked at the closet.

"It's okay, girl. I don't have to open this door." He tossed his coat across the chair beside the closet. "I'll just leave my coat here."

His answer was the little dog wagging her tail at him, waiting for an ear scratch that he gave her.

Happy now, Ginger trotted back into the kitchen.

"I'll have to get it out again when we watch the movie," Marcie said. "But it can stay in there until then."

Marcie had to admit she felt safer around that elf with Ted there.

She always felt safe around Ted.

If only he could stay here with me. Then if the elf moved again, he might catch whoever was moving it.

But she didn't ask him. Or tell him that the creepy elf now scared her.

CHAPTER 7

*M*arcie bit her lip.

It scared her that someone had been able to come in and move that elf.

That someone had known to put the elf in the cereal bowl area where they knew she'd see it before she had her breakfast.

It must be someone who knows me, or at least knows my habits. But why pick on me?

They went into the kitchen so she could finish baking the rest of the cookies.

"Did I tell you about my twin brother's wedding this month?" he asked.

His question took her mind off her worries.

He was good at that.

"You just said that you needed a dog-sitter and you were going to be in the wedding," she said. "You haven't said much about your twin, at all."

"I'm the best man so I'll fly out for that. But it's just a weekend event."

"What does your brother do in Montana?" she asked, her mind conjuring up cowboys, and rodeos, and ranching.

"He's in private security. The group is called Brotherhood Protectors," he said. "The guys are all former military, with special skills. The group is based in Eagle Rock, Montana."

"I've never heard of Eagle Rock," she said.

"I hadn't either," he said, "before Jack took the job and moved out there. It's not a large place. They're getting married on a ranch."

"Cool," she said. "So, like a cowboy wedding? With hats and boots, and all?"

"No, I don't think so," he said. "I'll be wearing a tux, but no mention was made of hats or boots. And black dress shoes to go with the tux."

"You'll be so handsome," she said. "I'll want to see pictures."

He smiled at her. "Sure," he said.

"Will lots of your family be there?" she asked.

"Our parents are flying in for the wedding," he said. "Then they'll head out on their travels."

"That will be nice," Marcie said. "Like a family reunion."

"Our family reunions are huge," Ted said. "If all the cousins attend. Many of them are deployed, so that's not easy. Jack's wedding will be smaller than our reunions."

"I envy you the family reunions," Marcie said. "I've always wanted a big, loving family. You are lucky."

"True," he said. "I am."

She began fixing a plate of cookies for them to nibble on tonight, and another plate for Ted to take home with him.

He sampled more than one cookie, snuck kisses in-between which took her mind off her troubles and teased her about how hungry he was.

Marcie's mind was now more on kissing Ted than on baking cookies.

A small kiss here, a small kiss there, had her yearning for his touch ... and his kisses.

As she pulled the last tray of cookies out of the oven and placed it on top of the cooling rack to cool, he slid his hands around her waist and bent in to kiss her on the neck, below her right ear.

Goosebumps spread down her neck, and her body heated.

His hands pulled her hips back toward him, and his warm hands rested on her hips.

"Do you have any other place you'd like me to kiss?" he whispered in her ear.

"Oh yes," she breathed.

"Good," he kissed her below her ear again and then gave it a nibble. "I want you to show me. Tell me."

She pulled away, and, taking him by the hand, said, "I need to shower all this sugar and flour off. It's even in my hair. Let's go upstairs."

"Okay," he said. "You lead."

Feeling bold, and liking the feeling of being in charge, she led him up the stairs and into the bathroom.

"You can wash my back and I will wash yours," she said.

It was the boldest she'd ever been with a man, but something about being with Ted was bringing a new side of her out. A bolder side.

She started to undress.

"Let me help you," he said.

He took hold of her T-shirt and pulled it over her head before kissing her again.

He continued kissing her until her clothes were off, and his as well.

She let her eyes roam over his naked body.

He was even more fit than she had imagined. His abs alone made her want to touch him, to feel those toned muscles.

Moving toward the shower he turned it on and adjusted the water to warm.

Then kissing her again, he moved them both into the shower.

As the water coursed down her body, he began to move his lips down from hers, kissing her lower and lower.

She closed her eyes, and leaned her head back, letting herself relax and enjoy every blissful moment.

They made love until the warm water ran out.

Finally clean, and finished making love, they dried each other off, which led them to start kissing all over again.

"I could kiss you all night," he said.

Marcie laughed. "Eventually we will have to get to the movie."

"If you insist," he said. "As you wish."

The reference to a favorite line from one of her favorite movies, The Princess Bride, made her smile.

Ted was everything she could have wished for and more.

MARCIE FOUND a popcorn popper in the kitchen after she first arrived, but no popcorn kernels on the shelves.

So, she'd bought a big tin of already-popped popcorn at the grocery store. The tin held three kinds of popcorn to choose from—caramel, cheddar, and regular.

She'd get out the ready-made popcorn to take the elf picture and would pretend it was freshly popped.

Then, she and Ted would enjoy the specialty popcorn, with the movie.

Beverly's instructions, and insisting on certain things, is silly.

None of this elf stuff is real, anyway.

It was all made up.

"Once the pictures are out of the way, we can relax and just watch the movie," she said.

"Sounds good to me," Ted said. "Want to cuddle on the couch?"

"I would love to," she said.

Cuddling up to watch the movie sounded like a perfect evening, after making love in the late afternoon.

"Ginger, would you like some popcorn?" she asked the little dog, who was sniffing at the tin of popcorn. "It does smell good, doesn't it?"

Ginger wagged her tail and barked once.

"I'll take that as a yes," Marcie laughed.

She held out her hand, giving Ginger a few pieces.

Once Ginger took the last one, and licked Marcie's palm, tickling it, Marcie giggled.

"She's a good companion for you," Ted said.

"Yes, she is," Marcie said. "I love dogs."

"Me too," he said. "I waited a long time to get Ace because I travel so much. But I'm stationed stateside now."

"That's good," she said. "Ace is a great dog."

"He is," Ted said. "He was a military dog; I got him from an organization that finds homes for them after their service. He's deaf in one ear, but that doesn't hinder him in civilian life. And I'm loud enough." He laughed.

"Oh, what a great thing to do," she said. "I'm happy you found each other."

"Me, too." Ted smiled. "Ready to watch the movie?"

He had the movie set up, so it was ready to go.

"Yes. I'm ready to get this elf picture out of the way, so I can put the creepy elf back in the closet and start to relax."

Ted gave her a thumbs-up.

Marcie got the elf out of the closet again, as Ginger barked and growled at it.

Ted went into the kitchen for more cookies while she got a picture with the elf watching the movie, texted it to Beverly, and put the elf away again.

Ginger was quiet after growling one last growl, before the closet door was closed.

"It's a lot quieter here, when that elf is put away," Marcie said. "That elf causes nothing but stress."

"Come here, baby," Ted sat on the couch and held out his arms. "Come over here and cuddle and forget about that old elf."

"Okay," she said.

Soon, they were cuddled up on the couch, watching the movie, as Ted held her close.

The nearness made her feel at peace, without a care in the world, the elf and her employer forgotten.

She loved being held in his arms.

It only we could stay here forever, just like this.

She tried to hold onto the feelings because she knew they couldn't last.

Eventually, she would have to get on a plane and fly back to her home base in Ohio. Which she really didn't want to think about.

She focused on Rudolph, and his problems with his glowing nose.

It was a good movie.

One she'd enjoyed since she was a child.

Halfway through the movie, Marcie felt Ginger's cold, wet nose nudging her hand.

Marcie petted her and scratched her behind the ears, with Ginger leaning into her hand, liking it.

The little dog probably liked it as much as Marcie liked leaning on Ted.

"Everyone gets some loving tonight," she told Ginger, who woofed.

When the movie was over, Ted and Marcie made out on the couch, until they lost track of time. But eventually they both needed to come up for air.

"I love kissing you," he said. "The way you taste so sweet, and I love your silky-smooth hair and soft skin."

"I love it when you kiss me, and touch me," she said. "I need to be touched."

"You were meant to be touched, and kissed," he said. "Loved on, and well loved."

She melted beneath his words, as she did beneath his kisses and his touch.

"I'm hoping to have the pleasure of your company this Christmas Eve," he said. "Or Christmas Day, depending on how you like to celebrate. I'm hoping you'll say yes to spending the holiday with me. The whole holiday. Day and night."

A soft smile spread across her face. "Yes. I'd love that. It's been a while since I spent Christmas with anyone, and I would love to spend it with you. Day and night."

Things were moving fast, but it felt right. Never had anything in Marcie's life felt so right.

She just knew Ted was her man, and she was his woman.

This was meant to be. So, the speed was not just okay, it was more than okay.

"As soon as I'm back from Montana," he said, "we'll make plans for the holiday."

"I can't wait," she said. "This will be the best Christmas ever."

~

Day nine: Elf is naughty – take a bite out of one of the cookies and put it back on the plate.

MARCIE CHECKED THE LIST.

Today's task was easy.

All she had to do was send the photos she'd taken Sunday night, when she and Ted were eating cookies and watching the movie.

She'd decided it was less stressful to go ahead and take the photos before they were needed and then send them on the day they were scheduled rather than ahead of time.

If she didn't know Marcie had taken the photos early, then she was less likely to lose it and start yelling at Marcie via text messages.

~

ZEKE KINGSLEY PULLED a receipt from his jacket pocket, looked down at it, and then, realizing what it was for, chuckled.

This is going to be fun.

He tore the receipt into small pieces as he thought of all the surprises he had in store for the hot little blonde, Marcie Hayes.

"Zeke?" Beverly called from the other room. "Is that you?"

He threw the pieces in the trashcan, buried them

beneath some goopy kitchen trash that Beverly would never touch, and then moved toward the kitchen sink.

"Yes, darling," he called as he washed his hands, "I'm home."

"I've been waiting for you," Beverly sang.

He'd just bet she was.

Probably wearing some slinky nightgown which she thought was sexy.

He was less than impressed with the slinky designer label stuff.

If only she'd try wearing something see through, for a change.

He needed to see and watch to get excited.

But the one time he'd brought it up, Beverly acted like he had suggested something terrible.

Seeing the look on her face made him decide never to ask her again.

He moved toward the bedroom in their condo, where Beverly was already in bed.

Beverly would never know it was the curvy blonde whom he'd found to dog- and house-sit for her who was on his mind when they made love.

He thought again of watching Marcie's tits bounce.

Half the thrill was having a girl on the side who nobody else knew about, as well as the anticipation of taking a girl and making her his.

Getting away with having a side girl while also having Beverly gave him an extra thrill, as this was new, and he liked putting one over on Beverly who'd lately become more demanding, now that they'd been dating for a year.

She thought of him as hers.

But he would never belong to anyone, especially a woman.

Women belonged to him, not the other way around.

No woman had told him what to do since his mama, and no woman ever would. Once his mama had been buried in the ground, he had buried that kind of thing forever.

Beverly wasn't as smart as she thought she was.

If she got too far out of line, he would see that she was buried too.

Now that he had a well-connected girlfriend, he couldn't simply leave her; with her many social connections there would be repercussions if she took up against him.

He needed to keep her under control for her own good. It would be a shame to have to do away with her that way.

He brushed that thought aside and focused on the woman reclining on the bed.

"Roll over," he said, "I'll rub your back."

She did as he asked because she knew he would make her feel good.

He could continue his thoughts without having her watching his face.

She'd been his girlfriend for over a year.

Living an ordinary social life with her, presenting the false front to the world that he needed. She was arm candy for the social pages.

If not for her big tits and long blonde hair, which he enjoyed wrapping his hand around and yanking hard to make her hold still, he wouldn't have bothered with Beverly.

He wouldn't yank on her hair because she would say that was too rough.

She'd been a pampered little girl and now expected to be pampered as an adult woman, too. The key to Beverly was providing that expected pampering.

Beverly was for the world to see.

His side girls were private.

And his girlfriend had no idea about the other women.

No one did. They were his dirty little secret.

Marcie would be his fourth, and the first girl to have on the side since he got with Beverly.

He had waited a long time to find another girl as he'd had to make sure all his focus was on his new society girlfriend at first. He'd made sure to seem to be the man of her dreams.

Zeke continued rubbing her back and occasionally whispering an endearment, to make her think he had her on his mind.

Tonight, he would have to behave, while being bored out of his mind and forced to keep thinking of the bouncing tits he'd seen earlier on the video.

He had to keep Beverly happy.

She was his alibi if he ever needed one.

Smiling to himself, he thought about the blonde and the footage he had taken already.

The girl was perfect. Young, blonde, full tits, curvy, pretty eyes, and full lips. No family, and all alone for the holiday.

I can keep her forever. No one will ever miss her.

"Zeke," Beverly moaned, impatient now, wanting him to do more.

"Yes, dear," he said, kissing her shoulder and then rolling her over to face him.

He kept his mind on the image of Marcie's bare bouncing tits and proudly showed Beverly just how eager he was.

"Oh, Zeke," Beverly reached for him. "Take me to paradise."

Nodding to her, he positioned himself, ready.

She had no idea what paradise really was. He was the one headed for paradise.

Just a few more days until his 'business trip' to his Manhattan office.

Just a few more days until those tits, and everything that came with Marcie, would be beneath his hands and tied to the big iron bed in the old cabin he'd purchased with a shell company a few years ago.

Christmas would come early for him this year.

He put on a big smile for Beverly, gave her a wink, and said, "Hey, baby, are you ready?"

She appeared pleased, as she thought his excitement was all for her.

Day ten: Elf writes letter to Santa.

MARCIE MADE UP A LETTER, from the elf, which went like this:

Dear Santa,

This is Tananna. Don't worry. I'm not in jail this year. I am not in any trouble. It's hard to get into trouble when you are locked in a coat closet, every night. Maybe you should have the doll-makers give me a nicer-looking face. Small dogs are afraid of me and bark. Ginger, the little dog who lives here, does not like me at all. She barks and barks. Hurry to our house. We have fresh cookies for you.

Signed,

Tananna Elf

For fun, she addressed the letter to Santa at the North Pole and put a stamp on it.

She wouldn't let Beverly read what the letter said. This one was for her private fun.

The photo she took for the contest only showed the elf

having written 'Dear Santa' with a black pen on the fancy Christmas stationery Beverly had bought for this letter-writing task.

It was good quality paper, and it seemed a shame to waste it, so Marcie had finished the letter for fun and got it ready to go out in the mail to Santa.

Sometimes she was still very much a kid, at heart.

It was a shame she had no one to share that joy with.

But joy spent alone could still be joy.

As if he had read her thoughts, or knew she was suddenly thinking of him, Ted called her, and she picked up.

"Hello," she said, happy to hear from him.

"How's it going?" he asked.

"Good," she said. "It's day ten, since I got here, so it's laundry day for me. I got the silly elf photo out of the way."

"So, day ten is laundry day. Check," he said. "Your time here is going fast."

"It is," she said. "So is yours, especially with the upcoming wedding."

"I called to see if you wanted to go into town with me today to do some shopping," he said.

"If I had clean, dry socks, I would," she said. "But they are currently in the washing machine which just filled up with water." She sighed. "They are literally all wet and sort of stinky."

He laughed and she laughed with him.

"Tomorrow let's go find you some new socks," he said. "It's best to have extra pairs on hand. Ask any military guy or gal and they will tell you that."

"Okay," she agreed. "Tomorrow, I'll go sock shopping with you. If that's really what you want to do."

"It is," he said. "I want to make sure you are well stocked

before I leave, with wood for the fireplace, warm socks, and anything else you might need, in case you get snowed in while I am gone."

"That's sweet of you, Ted," Marcie said.

"Just looking after my girl," he said.

Marcie giggled.

It was so nice to be looked after by Ted.

Who would have thought, in the Pocono Mountains, with hardly anyone around, that she would have found such an awesome boyfriend.

It must be the military training he'd had, as he tended to constantly do things for her safety and wellbeing, unlike other boyfriends she'd had.

She liked that ... a lot.

"Nine a.m. if you want to have breakfast at the diner on the way or 10 a.m. if you'd rather eat breakfast before I pick you up."

"I'd rather have breakfast with you," Marcie said.

"Then I'll see you at nine."

"Yes, see you then."

Marcie floated through the rest of her otherwise boring, mundane day doing laundry, dishes, and cooking dinner for herself, with thoughts of how much fun she would have tomorrow, going shopping with Ted.

Time spent with Ted was always fun. She was really going to miss him when he flew to Montana for the wedding.

Day eleven: Take a picture of the elf upstairs in bed with you, reading a bedtime Christmas story. Be sure to wear cute pajamas.

MARCIE READ the list for today's task and rolled her eyes.

Not happening.

At least not the way Beverly wanted.

Cute pajamas.

Marcie usually slept in a T-shirt and panties, or her white silk nightgown. She didn't own one pair of cute pajamas. And she wasn't about to buy some just to take a picture.

Even if she was going shopping with Ted today.

How much did that woman expect her to spend on things for these pictures?

No way would the extra fifty dollars cover new pajamas and the other things she'd had to buy if she did what Beverly wanted.

She glanced out the window, her stomach growling.

Ted would be here soon, and she was ready for breakfast. Had been for half an hour now.

Luckily, the drive to the diner wasn't far.

The drive into Scranton to go shopping would take an hour.

She yawned, having woken up too early this morning, excited about their day together.

I hope I don't fall asleep in the car again. He's going to think that's all I ever do when he drives me somewhere.

She watched him pull his car into the drive and waved. Then she hurried to get her coat on before she opened the door.

When she opened the door, he grinned widely. "You must be hungry," he said.

"I am," she nodded. "And I woke up early."

Having breakfast with Ted beat having oatmeal alone, hands down.

Even though having Ginger watching her eat wasn't exactly alone.

"Great," he said, taking her elbow as she stepped out onto the front porch. "Careful."

The mat had some snow and ice on it, which she noticed as she looked down.

Good thing he was looking out for her, as she tended not to notice things around her when he was near.

Her attention instead went to him.

Somehow, he was always vigilant and aware. Likely that military training thing again.

Ted always being aware made her able to relax and not have to pay as much attention to her surroundings as she usually did.

"Have you eaten at the diner before?" she asked as he walked her to the passenger side.

"Nope. But I hear it's good food," he said.

"Well, it's kind of hard to mess up eggs," she said.

"It can happen." He shook his head. "A bad mess cook can ruin about anything. And MREs aren't all that exciting." He reached into his jacket pocket. "Hence the ever-present Tabasco sauce." She laughed. "For real?"

"Oh yeah." He nodded as he pulled it out of his pocket and waved it.

. "If you know anyone serving overseas, ask if they'd like some in a care package. I'll bet they say yes."

"Wow," she said. Then she squinted at him as the morning sun was bright. "So, you guys travel with food stuff, kind of like I do."

"Many of us do. What and how much is a personal thing."

"What foods do you always have?"

"Tabasco for starters," he said, tapping the Tabasco

bottle. "And old-fashioned lemon drops." He reached back into his pocket and pulled out two lemon drops. "What my grandpa always carried. He was in the Army."

"So, it's a tradition," she said.

He held out his hand with the lemon drops and offered her one. "Skipped a generation, and my twin doesn't do lemon drops, but yes," he said.

She took the lemon drop. "Thank you."

"Welcome," he said.

"What does your twin do, for carry with him food? He's in the Marines, right?"

"Beef jerky and Red Hots candies," he said. "And yes, he's a Marine."

"Do you like those two things as well?"

"Only the jerky," he said. "Jack and I are alike mostly in looks. As kids, we didn't like or want everything the same, like matching shirts or stuff like that. He always wanted red, and I wanted blue."

"So, you were trying to be different from each other," she said.

"Yes, but we also genuinely liked those things," he said. "Especially once we reached college age, and everything wasn't a reaction to someone else."

"You outgrew that once you grew up."

"Pretty much," he said. "And we're close. Don't get me wrong. We like fishing and hunting together. Skiing. He'll probably want to come out here and bring his new wife to check out my new place, once they are done honeymooning. I offered them the place for a weekend getaway when I'm not using it. I hope my whole family will come out eventually."

"Maybe next Christmas?" she said.

"Maybe."

The one-hour drive seemed to fly by and soon they were in Scranton, shopping at a department store for socks.

He, being of a more practical nature, talked her into some good, thick hiking socks.

She bought ones with just a bit of pink in them.

And then she saw what she could only think of as the star socks.

Dark blue socks with white stars on them, reminding her of the night sky. They were soft, they were pretty, the kind you might wear around the house instead of slippers, and they were also as much for one pair as the sets of three she had been looking at.

Very impractical, but she loved them. Her eyes lit up and she let a finger linger on one of the soft socks before letting her hand drop and then walking past them.

"I have a bit of a dilemma," Marcie said, taking her mind off the socks and wanting to tell him about the dilemma she had.

Ted paused to look down at her. "What's your dilemma?"

"I'm supposed to take a picture tonight in bed with the elf," she said. "And I'm really not comfortable with my picture in bed floating all around the internet."

He frowned. "I'm not either," he said. "If you're going to do it, we'll have to crop off your head. There's a lot of crazies out there and, Marcie, if no one has told you before, you are a beautiful woman. Pictures of you would draw attention from men."

"Thank you." She blushed, the heat in her face rising. "I like your idea of chopping off my head."

A lady ahead of them who was shopping, turned and gave them each a sharp glance.

"In a photo," he said to the woman with a laugh. "No axes will be involved, I promise."

The lady nodded and then turned back around to continue her shopping.

"Anyway," Marcie said, "I'm supposed to wear cute pajamas, but I don't even own pajamas, cute or otherwise. So, I'm just going to wear a long T-shirt and leggings instead."

"Sounds like a plan," he said with a smile.

Her shopping complete, she checked out with her socks. They were headed for the exit when she said, "Oh, I need to run to the ladies' room and can't take this bag in with me. Can you hold it for me?"

"Of course," he said.

She handed the bag to him and headed toward the restroom.

Inside, she wanted to hurry, but there was a line. When she came out, he was waiting for her in a different spot than where she had left him, but she saw him right away and went over to him.

"All set?" he asked.

"Yes," she said.

"Nothing else you need?"

"I have everything I need," she said with a smile.

"How about Italian at our favorite place, an early dinner, before we head back," he said.

"That sounds good to me."

They drove to the Italian restaurant which had been their second date and this time they ordered a big pizza with pepperoni, olives , and mushrooms.

It was more of a late lunch/early dinner as they had spent many hours shopping. Stocking his lake house for the holidays required him to get a lot of things now that he had stocked the basics there.

Christmas decorations, several couch throws to warm up under, picture frames to go on the fireplace mantel which he would fill with family photos, and Christmas surprises for Ace.

Marcie had enjoyed helping him select things.

He'd insisted she pick the couch throw that she liked best.

One side was soft and velvety and the other looked like soft sheep fur but wasn't. It was blue-and-green plaid; she'd been drawn to the colors and how soft it looked.

They were both shopped out, and hungry.

The pizza was delicious, but they couldn't eat it all, so when they were done they asked for a to-go box to take the leftovers home.

"Two boxes," she said.

"One," he said. "I'll let you keep it. Since I fly out tomorrow."

It made her nervous that he was leaving.

Someone had come into the house and moved that elf. Now he was going out of town so she couldn't call him to come over.

What would she do if the person came back?

But she couldn't ask him to stay. He had to go to the wedding. And she couldn't go with him.

She wouldn't have been bold enough to ask to go with him, and even if she had been, who would watch the dogs?

No, he had to go, and she had to stop thinking like a frightened rabbit.

Nothing has happened since that one time the elf moved. Hopefully nothing else will happen. He's only going to be gone for the weekend.

CHAPTER 8

*T*ed was still talking about the pizza, unaware that her mind had drifted.

"Maybe you'll share a slice, if I come over again between now and then."

"Of course," she said. "I'll always share my pizza with you."

Big, flat snowflakes were falling so he turned on the radio to hear the weather report.

Flurries all night and into the morning. Nothing so bad as to delay his flight though, or to snow them in.

The temperature was dropping; it would be a cold night.

"I'm glad you convinced me to buy new socks," she said. "Mine were kind of worn out and I confess, a few have holes in them."

He gave her a look. "You didn't tell me that. We should have bought you more."

"They're still wearable," she said with a shrug. "They aren't that bad."

"Wear the new ones, not the old ones, when you go outside," he said. "They'll keep your feet warm and dry."

"Yes, sir."

Geesh, I have never heard him take that tone with me before. All commanding and stuff.

Deep down, she kind of liked it. Liked that he cared enough about her to want her to keep her feet warm and dry.

What guy she gone out with had ever come close to caring about something like that?

To really caring about her good health and general welfare.

Not one.

"I like my new socks," she said. "Thank you again for guiding me to buy that kind."

"The pretty ones you were looking at aren't made for trekking through snow," he said.

"No," she said. "They aren't. They're better for inside."

They enjoyed the rest of the trip back and soon he was pulling into the driveway to park.

"I'll bet Ginger needs out," she said.

"Ace will too, so I'm going to see you inside, make sure the place is secure, and then head on home," he said. "But if you need me for anything, call me."

"I will," she said.

He unlocked her door, walked through the place, checking locks and windows, while she let Ginger out of her crate and clipped her leash on.

"Come on, girl," Marcie said. "Time to do your business before the snowfall gets worse."

The little dog hesitated to step onto the snow, though Marcie knew that she needed to go. At last, she coaxed her out.

Ginger quickly went and then woofed to go back inside.

"Good girl," Marcie praised the little dog and reached

into her coat pocket for a small treat, which she gave to her, before letting her back inside.

"You're all set," Ted said, as he met Marcie on the front porch. "Lock this door once I'm gone."

"I always do," Marcie said.

"And no keys under the mat," he said.

"No keys under the mat," Marcie agreed.

He came over to her and kissed her goodbye. "I'm going to get packed and spend some time with Ace tonight. But I'll get back over here tomorrow before I leave."

"Okay," she said. "Give Ace an ear scratch or a belly rub for me."

"Will do."

He got into his car, backed it down the driveway, and drove off.

She went into the house, and as she closed and locked the door behind her, she was glad the key was no longer under the mat.

LATER THAT NIGHT, as she opened the shopping bag to get out her new socks, she saw another smaller bag inside.

Marcie pulled the smaller bag out and dumped the contents on the bed.

Star socks.

She gasped.

He'd seen her look at them, and knew she wanted them.

Though neither she nor he had said a word about it, he'd bought them for her, as a surprise.

She reached for her phone and dialed his number.

"Marcie? You okay?" His concerned voice came on the line.

"I am more than okay," she said. "I am over the moon about these star socks. I can't believe you got them for me! You didn't have to do that."

"I wanted to," he said.

"Well, I love them," she said. "Thank you. I am going to wear them tonight."

And every night until you come home.

She kept that thought to herself.

"You're welcome," he said. "I'm glad you like them."

"They are awesome, and so are you," she said.

He cleared his throat, as if he was a little choked up.

"Thanks," he said quietly.

Did he get choked up? There's so much to learn about him still.

But she liked everything she had learned so far.

"Enjoy them," he said. "I've got to finish packing."

"Oh, right," she said. "I don't want to keep you from it. I'm going to get on with taking this stupid elf photo."

"Without showing your head," he said.

"Right," she agreed. "No head. Check."

"I'll call you later, sweetie," he said.

"Okay, bye for now."

She put her phone on the charger and got ready to take a shower.

After she got dressed, she would go downstairs and get the elf out of the closet.

Ginger was not going to like that.

She had already been pouting after Marcie was gone all day shopping with Ted.

During her shower, Marcie let the memories of the day play through her head. Then she got out, dried off, and prepared for the photos in the bedroom she was sleeping in.

Earlier, she had solved the pajama dilemma by deciding to wear a soft T-shirt and leggings, hoping they would pass.

If not, she was going to tell Beverly that she couldn't do this one.

She didn't have the right clothing for the job.

For the story, she picked out *The Night Before Christmas*. Then she got the elf out of the closet without Ginger seeing it and brought both items upstairs for the photo.

Setting up the tripod on the dresser, it took several tries before she got a good shot.

Then she texted it to Beverly.

The photo must've been okay because she didn't hear a word back from her this time.

Ted called before she got into bed and drifted off to sleep.

He said he'd stop by early in the morning before he headed to the airport. He would leave her his spare key so she could get in to take care of Ace while he was away.

He hadn't even left yet, but already she was wishing he didn't have to go.

They had so little time left together before her house-sitting job was over and then she would be the one who had to leave.

But she tried not to think about that.

She would spend the weekend reading. That would help keep her mind off things, like elves that moved mysteriously and how much she was missing her new boyfriend.

A good story could make you forget anything.

As he stared at the picture, Zeke was furious.

But he couldn't let Beverly know.

He went over to the sideboard to pour himself a large glass of whiskey, so she wouldn't see his expression.

Could the little house-sitter not follow directions? Or was she willful and stubborn by nature?

The picture Marcie had texted was not of her in pajamas, or anything remotely sexy.

Instead, she was wearing a huge T-shirt which hid everything, and leggings beneath it.

What showed up large in the photo, being the closest thing to the camera, were fluffy dark socks with white stars.

Star socks. Like something a twelve-year-old would wear.

She looks like a child! Dressed like that.

That is not how she's supposed to look.

He fumed as he sipped, the anticipated of seeing and watching her in sexy pajamas ruined.

He didn't want to see her look like a child.

Like a child!

You couldn't see her nice full breasts enough in that huge T-shirt to know she had them.

His fantasies didn't revolve around children and the thought of Marcie dressing like a child was repulsive to him.

He needed her to look like the curvy woman she was.

She'd even cropped her head in the photo so he couldn't see her pretty face.

And now the elf had been put away again, so he was not getting to watch her on the video like he'd originally planned.

The stupid little dog of Beverly's didn't like the elf, that's why Marcie had to put it up.

He had to admit, he couldn't stand all that barking either. He didn't blame her for putting the elf away.

But now she was thwarting him by not following the instructions that had been left for her.

She'd better follow them tomorrow night.

If she doesn't, I will just go and take her.

I could go take her later tonight once I can break free from Beverly.

But no. Then there'd be no footage of Marcie's beautiful naked body in the bathtub.

I must have that.

Those round titties rising out of the bubbles in the bathtub, and then everything below.

The first time he would see her totally naked.

He calmed down, sipped on his whiskey again, and smiled to himself.

The cabin he'd bought had no bathtub, but he'd had a simple shower installed.

With those clear walls, there was nothing to block his view of her.

Once he had her inside the cabin, he could view her as often as he pleased, from any angle he chose.

He would make her wear what he chose, or she would wear nothing at all.

Soon. I will have her soon.

He turned on the video of her bouncing titties again. The only video of her showing anything which could get him excited.

Day twelve: Elf in the bathroom, with bubbles in the bathtub. We will call this — all clean children go on Santa's good list.

TED RAN by the house in the morning, to see Marcie before heading to the airport. He left her a key and instructions for taking care of Ace. Then he kissed her long and hard before he got in his car to leave.

He got to the airport just in time and boarded the plane. He took out his phone to call Marcie one more time. He wanted to talk to her before his plane took off.

Things would get busy once he landed.

Jack was picking him up at the airport. There wouldn't be much quiet time this weekend, with all the wedding events, to be in touch with her.

As the best man, he needed to be there for his brother.

It had been a long time since he'd seen Jack, and it pleased him that his brother had asked him to be best man in his wedding.

Ted had considered asking Marcie to go with him, but they'd just started dating.

Too soon to start introducing her to family.

Plus, she was house- and dog-sitting and couldn't have left town, anyway.

He dialed her number.

"Hello," she answered.

"Hey, babe," he said. "Just boarded the plane."

"Have a safe trip, and have fun," she said.

"Thanks. I will," he said. "How about dinner at that Italian place we like when I get back?"

"Sounds perfect," she said. "I still have a couple slices of pizza left."

"Good," he said. "Enjoy them. I'll see you soon."

"I can't wait to see you again," she said.

"Ditto," he said. "Talk to you later."

"Ditto," she said, with a laugh.

After they hung up, Marcie texted him a happy face and a thumbs-up.

He smiled, sent her a happy face in return, and then turned his phone to airplane mode. He sat back in his seat and closed his eyes, waiting for the plane to take off.

Time to grab a nap.

What he usually did, when flying commercial.

IT WAS time to take the next elf picture.

"This is going to be good," Marcie said to Ginger. "I'll enjoy a luxurious bath."

She would enjoy herself, even if she did have to deal with that creepy elf.

She could enjoy bubbles in the bath once the pictures were done.

Best thing on the whole list, in Marcie's opinion.

Beverly had expensive bath stuff. The scent of roses rising from the tub was heavenly.

Not like the cheap stuff Marcie bought at the drugstore.

This would be pampering. Something Marcie didn't do often.

Marcie placed the drain plug in the tub, then turned on the hot water.

She was looking forward to soaking and relaxing in the tub.

Getting the water to the right temperature, she then slipped a large, rose-colored bath bomb into the tub, holding it beneath the water filling the tub as it dissolved, and the old-fashioned scent of roses filled the air.

Oh, that smells so nice, she thought, as it melted in her hand, dissolving in the water.

When the bubbles were just so, she sat the elf on the edge of the tub and took a picture with the bubbles in the background.

Then she sat the elf beside the sink, where it wouldn't get wet.

Marcie undressed, taking off her sweater and then her jeans, standing in her bra and bikini panties.

She glanced in the mirror, trying to decide whether to leave her hair pulled back.

The bath would be so much more relaxing if she let her hair down.

She pulled her ponytail holder off, letting her long blonde hair fall down her back, and placed the ponytail holder beside the elf.

Then she took a minute to brush her teeth.

Bending down, to take off her socks, she thought about painting her toenails with the sparkly red nail polish which she'd packed for Christmas.

Marcie pulled off her bra and panties, letting them drop to the floor.

Then she slipped into the warm bubble bath and let out a long sigh of contentment.

She ignored the elf which sat facing her, refusing to look at the creepy thing.

Ordinarily, she would have taken it downstairs as soon as she took the photos, and locked it away in the coat closet, but she hadn't wanted the bath to get cold before she got in it.

The water temperature was just right, and she really needed this nice hot bath to finally relax.

Something she hadn't truly done since someone had moved the elf.

She really did need to stop thinking about that if she was ever going to relax here again.

Marcie sank down into the water, up to her chin, and closed her eyes.

Ah. This is so nice. The one thing on that list of daily things that I can really enjoy.

She closed her eyes and leaned her head back against the tub.

JUST AFTER CLOSING THE DOOR, he put his key away, pulled off his boots and left them by the door, and then adjusted his ski mask.

Tiptoeing quietly in his socks, he went to Ginger's crate, opened the door, and gave her a doggie biscuit.

"Good girl," he whispered, scratching her ears. Then he closed the door again, and left her.

He mounted the stairs until he reached the top.

All was quiet, as it should be.

Quietly, quietly, he crept down the hall toward his prey until he stood in the doorway, watching her in the bathtub with her eyes closed, her blonde hair down, and a peaceful expression on her face.

She was beautiful. Worthy of a painting or a professional picture.

He preferred pictures but, had the situation been different and she a society lady, he would have gladly paid to have her portrait painted, just as she was now.

Completely unaware of him, she rested.

Silently, he tiptoed closer. Taking a bottle of chloroform from his pocket, he removed the cap to pour the drug onto a hand towel.

Swiftly, he stepped closer to her, bending down to cover her nose and mouth with the towel. He forced the towel over her face.

She gasped.

Gripping her head with both his hands, he held the towel over her mouth and nose, forcing her to breathe the chloroform in.

Good. She'll breathe the stuff in faster.

He stared at her through the mask as she began thrashing.

But he was much stronger than her and the drug was working.

He waited, watching her.

Blurry vision made her blink several times, fast. But her eyes didn't focus on him for more than a few seconds.

"I have wanted you, my pet, and watched you from afar," he laughed. "And now, tonight, I finally have you."

With his last words, her eyes closed.

Then she was out, as the drug had taken hold.

A sudden dead weight, she would have slipped under the water, if he hadn't kept a firm grip on her.

He was much stronger than he looked. Muscular beneath his tailored suits.

Transporting her would be easier now, because she would not be able to fight him.

The new issue to deal with was her drugged body, which was heavier from the dead weight of her being unconscious.

Also, she was currently naked, and wet, and it was cold and snowing outside.

He didn't want her getting cold in this weather and then getting sick.

Unlike the other three, he would make sure this one

lasted. He would take better care of this one and then she would last.

With each one he had learned.

Pulling her body up, he draped her over the side of the tub, her long blonde hair falling toward the floor.

He stood up for a minute to catch his breath.

Turning the elf to face the wall, he pulled his mask off. He was sweating beneath it and now that Marcie was unconscious, there was no chance of her seeing him.

Moving back to her, he lifted her completely out of the tub and laid her down on the floor gently, careful not to bang her head.

Leaving her there, he went into the bedroom, and pulled the big comforter off the bed to carry it back into the bathroom.

Then he dried her off carefully with a towel.

He dressed her in the large black baggy sweatshirt and large black sweatpants which he had brought for that purpose. He wrapped her hair around her head and then put a black toboggan on her head, tucking her hair inside. Thick, black, warm socks were next.

Zeke stood looking at her, satisfied he'd hidden her as best he could.

He wrapped the comforter around her. He didn't bother with shoes.

She wouldn't be walking anywhere, for a long time, and when she did, it would only be the few steps her captivity would allow, when he allowed it.

With his prize wrapped, so no one could see what he had inside the comforter, he went into the bathroom to put his mask on and stopped short.

The bottle of chloroform had fallen over, onto his face

mask and leaked so that the mask was now damp and smelling of the stuff.

Dammit.

He wouldn't dare put the mask back on now. He would just have to be careful.

Seeing the trash can had a plastic liner, he pulled it out of the can and put the mask into in, then twisted the bag and tied it in a knot. He slipped the bag into his pocket, and then headed back into the bedroom and lifted Marcie into his arms.

He carried her down the stairs to the first floor and then down to the basement, where he exited the back door.

Tri-level houses sucked, he decided.

Too damn many stairs.

Moving into the woods, he headed to his van, which was parked two streets over, on a stretch which had homes that were all rentals for the skiing crowd.

Next week those houses were rented and full through the rest of the season, but tonight the street was empty.

No one would notice his van parked there unless they drove down the street.

He had to go through the back woods to reach that street, so that no one in the occupied houses would see him.

She was heavy, but this was why he worked so hard at bench pressing. When he was younger, he'd found it more difficult to carry an unconscious woman. As with many things, he had learned and adapted.

Now he carried Marcie swiftly through the woods with no problems other than the damn comforter which kept trying to slide.

The material was just slippery enough that it was slipping off her legs, one of which was now sticking out.

He adjusted her and the comforter, to try to cover her better.

But this was why he had dressed her in black.

Reaching the van, he managed to slide the door open, and then laid her down on the back seat. He reached for a handcuff and cuffed her to the seat. Then he took a bandana and tied it around her mouth.

If she did happen to come to, before he drove them down the road, away from here, she wouldn't be going anywhere or able to scream loud enough for anyone to hear her, with that gag.

He checked to make sure she was breathing, and then he slid the van door closed and headed back to Beverly's house.

Tonight, once Marcie was secured in the old cabin, he would ditch the van by driving it off the road into a tree, making the wreck look like an accident, and then he would torch it.

He was wearing gloves. There would be no fingerprints and no reason to look for any.

They wouldn't think to do that.

Nobody cared about an old van like this one, which was why he bought it. He'd used cash and hadn't bothered with registering the vehicle or getting tags. It could not be traced back to him as there was no paper trail.

They wouldn't even think to look for the girl. No one would miss her.

He laughed out loud at the assured success of his plan.

After placing her inside the van, he headed back into the house to clean up any trace of him being there. It didn't take long as he'd been very careful when coming in and he'd been wearing gloves the whole time. The only thing he had taken off was the ski mask.

Once back inside the house, he set to work cleaning up the mess he'd made.

He pulled the drain out of the tub, dried the bathroom floor, and then hung the wet towel on the towel bar. Glancing around, nothing looked out of place.

Taking the elf, he carried it into the bedroom and then sat it on the dresser, where it faced the bed.

He didn't want to waste time taking the camera out of the elf, because he would have to remove the stitching and then stitch the doll up again so no one would notice what he'd done.

He'd thought of taking the elf with him, but then he realized that though Beverly hadn't wanted the elf around, she would still wonder where the elf had gone, and there would be drama. That would draw too much attention to the elf.

The attention needed to be on how Marcie had flaked out on Beverly and hadn't finished her job. How she had probably hooked up with some ski bum and gone off with him. How unreliable she was.

Even if he took her the elf, there was no way now, for Beverly to win the contest because Marcie would not be taking any more photos to text to Beverly.

If the contestants failed to post a picture each day, they were automatically eliminated from winning.

It would happen to Beverly soon. But she couldn't know that.

Ginger was whining and giving him the quiet woof, which meant she needed to go out.

He didn't need her to start barking, so he let her out of her crate, got her leash and then took her outside to pee.

In a hurry once she was done, he let her back in and

opened the door to the bathroom. He tossed a toy inside and, when she followed it in, closed the door.

Now he needed to hurry back to the van and get on the road.

On Zeke's last pass through the kitchen, he grabbed an ornament Christmas cookie with red sugar sprinkled on top.

He took a bite as he went out the front door and locked it behind him.

Delicious.

He smiled.

I love Christmas.

CHAPTER 9

*D*ozing during most of the flight, Ted didn't wake until the captain's voice came over the speaker.

Soon, they had landed, and the plane was heading to the gate.

He turned his phone back on.

Jack had left a message.

"Hey, Bro, change of plans. I can't pick you up, so you'll need to pick up a rental car at the airport."

He called Marcie again. Her phone went to voicemail.

"Hey, Marcie, just landed," he said, leaving a message. "We didn't pick a time for dinner. How does six o'clock sound? Text me back when you can. Or call. Jack can't pick me up, so I've got to get a rental car and drive the rest of the way. Which would give us time to talk if you're free."

He didn't go into all the why, just wanted to let her know he'd be driving, not texting. He could always put her on speakerphone if the rental car didn't have a hands-free setup.

Ted got off the plane and went to the baggage claim area to collect his suitcase before heading for the rental car place. It might be slim pickings since he hadn't reserved one ahead of time and would have to go with what they had on the lot.

Then he would have to drive from Bozeman, Montana, to Eagle Rock, which appeared to be out in the middle of nowhere.

But that was where he had to go for the rehearsal and the rehearsal dinner afterward. Eagle Rock, Montana, where the wedding was being held at the Triple C Ranch.

Their original plan had been for Jack to pick him up and then they would head to the Triple C Ranch for the rehearsal.

Ted would freshen up and change clothes at the ranch, and then after dinner he'd drive back to his brother's apartment in Bozeman, where he would crash on the couch.

Hopefully, Jack had a good sleeping couch.

Much as he would have liked to spend more time with his brother, Jack, Ted preferred having his own rental car and at this point he was contemplating finding a hotel room, somewhere nearby.

If there was time.

His brother was currently chasing after horse thieves, racing away from the ranch, doing that 'hero to the rescue' thing again. Thieves had stolen the Triple C Ranch horses, and he was the closest one to catching them.

Jack had found his bride that way. So, it wasn't all bad. But the chase he was on now could easily screw up the couple's carefully made wedding plans.

Ted wondered how Lucy was taking all of this. He hadn't met her yet, but he'd heard a lot about her. Soon, she'd be his sister-in-law. That would be different, as they had no sisters or girl cousins their age. Ted looked forward to getting to know her.

Hopefully, Lucy wasn't too upset with Jack right now, as this was just how Jack was.

Remembering the day Jack had pulled him out of the icy water, saving his life, when they were boys, that memory was just as vivid now as the day it had happened. As if those moments were frozen within him, never again to be forgotten.

It had changed both their lives.

Jack had been rescuing people and animals ever since.

It was no surprise to Ted when Jack went into the Marines and joined a search and rescue team. Now that he was no longer an active-duty Marine, Jack was working for Brotherhood Protectors, which did private security and was based out of Eagle Rock.

Ted had no doubt that if anyone could catch those horse thieves and get the horses, it would be Jack.

Either way, his twin had better get back in time for his own wedding.

He shook his head.

Right now, he did not envy his twin, not one bit.

Glancing at his phone again, he wished Marcie would call him back. She wanted to hear about the wedding, and he already had a lot to tell her. He also had a long drive ahead of him.

Trying once more to call her, when it went to voicemail this time, he opted not to leave a message and turned on a radio station as he drove out of Bozeman toward Eagle Rock.

Marcie didn't know where she was, only that her head hurt, and she felt groggy.

She squinted through blurry eyes at the brass bed she

was lying on and frowned, which made her head hurt even more.

When she released the frown, it helped some. She relaxed her eyes.

The shiny brass bed was one she didn't recognize. The sheets and blankets around her were warm.

Where am I? She wondered as the fuzziness in her head continued.

The warmth of the bed was too tempting.

She gave herself over to it, closed her eyes, and fell asleep.

TED ARRIVED JUST in time for the rehearsal, which had already been pushed back an hour, as they all waited for Jack to return from chasing the horse thieves.

Like dominoes that had, in turn, pushed back the rehearsal dinner.

Mr. and Mrs. Barr, Jack and Ted's parents, had arrived the night before and were staying at the local bed and breakfast in Eagle Rock, before flying to Florida tomorrow, after the wedding.

From there, they'd be off on a cruise ship, sailing in the Caribbean. Since they would have been already seen both of their sons at the wedding, they'd decided to go on their first cruise, a seven-day Christmas cruise.

Both sons resembled their dad, with their dark hair, brown eyes, handsome features, and tall bearing. Though Mr. Barr now had a heavier amount of gray through his hair, in the way that looked so good on older men.

Their mother's hair was a silvery color, which went well with her blue eyes. She was a short, medium-sized woman who dressed conservatively and wore a lot of silver jewelry on her fingers and wrists.

At the Triple C Ranch, everyone gathered in the great room.

The local minister was there, waiting. It would not take long to move through the quick rehearsal for tomorrow's wedding.

The regular furniture had been moved to storage to make room for the rented white wedding chairs for the guests.

Lucy would come down the hall, where the bedrooms were located, and would walk down the center aisle, created by the layout of the chairs.

A tall Christmas tree stood in the corner, between the fireplace and the front wall, with its windows, each window holding a wreath of fresh greenery and a red bow. The tree had red bows and red and white bulbs all over, with a white star on the top.

White candles with red and gold ribbons were placed throughout the room, and red and white poinsettias were scattered around the base of the fireplace.

Ted had to admit, the setting was beautiful and as perfect as if someone from the Hallmark channel had done the decorating.

Though he'd only watched three shows with his former girlfriend, because she loved those shows, he'd seen enough similarities in the settings to note a general theme and look that they all had.

ON THE WEDDING DAY, the women in the bridal party wore dark green velvet dresses with hoods. The men's rented tuxes had vests which matched the green of the dresses. The ladies held bouquets of red and white roses, with deep green greenery and ribbons.

The white wedding cake had red poinsettias with green leaves decorating the snow-white cake.

Jack shifted nervously from one foot to the other as he waited for his bride.

Ted nudged Jack with his elbow. "Nervous?" he said, low.

"Nah," Jack said and forced himself to stand still.

Soon the wedding march was playing.

Lucy emerged from the hallway, and she looked beautiful. She had a glow about her.

His brother was a lucky man.

Her dress, made with white lace, hugged her upper body, and allowed a hint of soft pale skin to peek through the lace which rose to her neck. Her long dark hair had been curled and fell in waves down her back, and she carried a bouquet of red and white roses with greenery. Her bouquet matched the other red and white roses.

But it was the smile on her face and the light in her eyes which were the most beautiful.

Jack's eyes met Lucy's and never wavered, the love shining in both of their eyes for everyone to see.

AT THE RECEPTION AFTERWARD, Ted sat watching the bride's cousin, Rose, on the dance floor, as he sent Marcie a text.

The wedding was beautiful. Wish you could have seen it. I couldn't take pictures because only the professional photographer was allowed to.

It was a long text, for him. Longer than he usually sent.

But Marcie had wanted him to take pictures of the

wedding, and since he couldn't, he didn't want her to be disappointed.

If she wasn't expecting to see any, she wouldn't be.

He wasn't about to tell her about Lucy's cousin, Rose, with the big breasts. But he grinned watching Rose dance.

Rose's dress was cut too small for her, and as she danced, her breasts threatened to spill out of the low-cut top any minute.

Of course, it brought her a lot of attention from all the military guys.

It would be hard for any man to look away from that.

His brother, Jack, being the exception, as he was captivated by his new bride and only had eyes for her.

That's not to say that he hadn't noticed Rose. Jack didn't miss much.

It was several minutes before Ted checked his phone again, as he'd allowed Rose to divert his attention, briefly.

Marcie still hadn't answered.

It's late. Maybe she went to bed early and is still sleeping.

Her lack of a response seemed odd, as it had been hours since he'd sent her the first text.

Even a busy person could squeeze in a few words.

But how busy can she be? She's just house-sitting in the Poconos and dog-sitting that cute little Cocker Spaniel, Ginger.

There's no one around who Marcie knows, other than me. She's never been to the Pocono Mountains before taking the job and we just met a few weeks ago.

Unless she met someone else right after I flew to Montana. Maybe she's made a new friend. Or a new boyfriend.

Still, she ought to answer him.

What seemed weird was how she'd gone from 'can't wait to see you,' to no answer at all.

He hoped nothing bad had happened.

Could she be sick? Unable to answer her phone? I hope she's all right.

He couldn't help but worry about her. She was all alone there.

What if something had happened to her?

WHEN TED still hadn't heard from Marcie the next morning, he looked up the phone numbers for the local police department for Gouldsboro, Pennsylvania.

Great.

He learned that Gouldsboro was a village, not a town, in Lehigh Township, and had only a part-time police department. He hoped they had enough officers and very little crime so they could send a car to check on her as soon as possible. He also hoped the officers were well trained.

Being out in Montana, two hours behind Pennsylvania, their offices would be open now.

He'd slept in after a late night and then made it to the hotel's free breakfast, ten minutes before they closed it down for the day.

He would try calling Marcie one more time, in the hope that he wouldn't need to call the police.

Surely, she'd be up by now and getting on with her day.

He tried her number again. No answer.

Something is wrong.

He felt it in his gut and dialed the police department right away.

A female answered the phone, and he wondered if she was a secretary or an officer. He hadn't wanted to tie up 911 by calling that number, with a small police department, in case somebody in the village was having an emergency.

He didn't know for sure whether Marcie being missing was an emergency yet.

She could just be out walking the dogs.

But even as he had that hopeful thought, something told him that she wasn't.

His feeling that something was wrong had grown with each hour that ticked past without her calling him back.

"Hello, can I get a wellness check?" he asked the dispatcher. "I'm very concerned about my girlfriend, Marcie Hayes. She hasn't been responding to texts for a couple days and that's unlike her. I'm worried something might be wrong."

"Did you have an argument? Any reason she might not want to talk to you?"

"No, nothing like that, but even if we had, she's also taking care of my dog, Ace, so she should have been stopping over at my place to feed him and take him for walks. She wouldn't ignore me like this."

"Okay," the dispatcher said. "We'll send a car by. Name and location?"

He rattled off the address and her name, then he gave them his address, in case she'd gone over there to take care of his dog. "Thanks for checking on her."

"No problem. We'll call you back after we check."

Thirty minutes later, when the police dispatcher called Ted back, she said, "We sent a patrol car by the house, but no one answered the door. There was a car in the drive, and we heard a dog barking."

"That would be Ginger, the Cocker Spaniel she's dog-sitting," Ted said.

"Same thing at your house. No one came to the door. Just the dog barking."

"Okay, well, thank you for checking."

"You're welcome," the dispatcher said.

There was nothing else he could do until he got home, except to keep trying to reach Marcie. Now he was anxious to get home to see what was wrong with his girlfriend and to check on the dogs.

But he had to go say goodbye to his parents and other relatives before they all flew back to their homes.

He hadn't mentioned Marcie to anyone yet, as she was such a new girlfriend that he didn't feel ready. So, he didn't have anyone to talk to about this development, though ordinarily he would have talked to his twin.

Normally, Jack may have even sensed that something had Ted very worried. But Jack and Lucy were already off on their honeymoon, and Ted was sure that he was the last person his twin would have on his mind for a while.

Which was just as a honeymoon should be. He hoped they were having the time of their lives, the first of many great moments together. He'd never seen Jack so happy.

Ted ended up giving his parents a ride to the airport, so they could make the most of their time together.

Hearing about their trip kept his mind busy, though thoughts of Marcie were always present and likely would be until he knew what was going on.

THE PLANE HAD FINALLY LANDED, and he turned his phone back on, hoping to see a call from Marcie. But there was nothing.

He hurried to the baggage area and stood impatiently waiting for his bag, wishing he hadn't had to check his bag, so he could have been out of there faster.

Collecting his bag, he jogged to the parking area to collect his Blazer.

Tossing his bag into the back seat, he prepared for the one-hour drive back home, remembering how every time he drove Marcie home from Scranton, she had dozed off and slept most of the way.

Odd quirk that it was, he missed her doing that. The passenger seat next to him felt empty and the car much too quiet.

He always had either Ace or Marcie in the car since he'd arrived in the Poconos. He wasn't used to being in this total silence.

Unable to take the quiet anymore, he reached to turn the radio on. He drove with the radio on and his cell phone next to his leg where he could grab it fast if Marcie or the police called.

An hour later, he pulled into his driveway and parked. Then he hurried to unlock his front door and check on Ace.

The moment Ted reached his home, he knew something was wrong.

Ace was barking loud and long, as if trying to tell him just how wrong, and when he unlocked the door and opened it, Ace dashed past him out into the yard to immediately do his business beside a tree.

No one had let him out for a while.

Standing with the door open, Ted glanced inside.

On the floor, to the right side of the door, was a puddle of urine. He knew Ace had held it as long as he could.

Ted hurried to the kitchen to look at the food and water bowls.

Empty.

When had she last been here?

He filled both bowls. Ace came back in and drank his water like he'd been out in the desert.

Had she been here at all? Even once?

His gaze went to the card for her on the dining room table, where it laid just as he'd placed it. Untouched, unopened.

Chills ran up his back.

She hadn't been here. There was no way in hell she would have neglected Ace.

Marcie loved dogs and fussed over them, and she was especially fond of his dog.

"Come on, boy!" Ted shouted.

Ace joined him racing to the car.

"We have to find Marcie."

Where is she?

CHAPTER 10

Ted drove as quickly as possible to the house where Marcie was house-sitting and parked.

Ace followed him out the car door. Jack left the door open as he hurried to the house.

He pounded on the front door.

"Marcie!" He yelled loud enough there was no way she would not have heard him.

He listened carefully but she didn't answer.

Barking came from the back of the house, not near the door.

Ginger is here, but not loose, or she would've been at the front door, barking.

His gut clenched, and he was even more sure that something was terribly wrong.

Experience had taught him that his gut was never wrong.

He needed to get inside. Now.

Not wanting to break into the house, he wished he had some way inside.

He stepped back, off the doormat and looked down.

Thinking that surely the house key, which had previously stayed under the doormat, would still be on her keyring where he'd put it himself not that long ago, he bent down and lifted the mat to check beneath it anyway.

His jaw dropped.

The key was back under the mat.

Dammit, Marcie! Why would you put the key back when I told you it wasn't safe?

He slipped his gloves off, picked the key up, and quickly used it to unlock the door.

Where is she? I hope she's okay.

The twisting in his gut told him she wasn't.

Opening the door, he called for her. "Marcie?"

No answer came, other than Ginger's excited barking, which was not coming from the room her crate was in.

He glanced around the front room, quick, and saw nothing out of order. Then he headed toward the barking to see to Ginger.

The little dog was in the first-floor bathroom, scratching at the closed door.

Ted opened the door and the excited little dog rushed out, barking, and jumping up on him. Something he'd never seen Ginger do.

Ginger did not jump up on people.

"Do you need to go out, girl?" He noticed the puddle on the bathroom floor. Like Ace, she hadn't been let out.

The little dog ran to the front door, and he followed, to keep an eye on her since she was off leash.

He stood, watching as she did her business.

Then she ran back to him.

"Come on, let's find Marcie," he said.

Woof.

The little dog was agreeable.

"Marcie?" he called out as Ginger trotted along next to him. Ace came inside and followed behind them.

Marcie didn't answer, confirming what he already knew, deep down.

She was gone.

Ted had to look for clues to where she might have gone. Maybe he would see something that the police wouldn't once he called them.

He climbed the stairs and headed for the main bedroom which had become Marcie's during her stay and stopped short, in shock.

The elf sat on the dresser, facing the bed. He frowned at it.

No way in hell would she have put that elf where it would sit and watch her in bed. Someone else had done this.

A chill ran down his back.

Someone else has been here and now she's gone.

"Where the hell is she?" he asked the elf, his voice turning into a growl.

But, of course, the antique doll couldn't answer him.

Ginger, having climbed up the stairs, entered the bedroom and started barking at the elf as soon as she saw it.

Not wanting to touch the elf, or anything else which the police might want to take prints off, he left it where it sat and tried to notice anything else unusual.

In the bedroom, her purse sat on the dresser and her phone was still plugged into the charger. She would have taken those with her.

His stomach clenched.

He looked at the phone to see her texts and phone calls.

Her last text had been to him.

She had no other texts, other than to Beverly. The only calls in and out were to or from him.

The sick feeling in his gut intensified.

How long has she been missing?

The police would ask him this question.

Though he saw no signs of a struggle, at first, he began to move more slowly, as he looked closer at everything in the bedroom and in the bathroom.

She'd run a bubble bath, which had left stuff on the sides of the tub. The room smelled like roses.

How long ago had she taken that bath? Was that something a CSI could figure out?

No puddles were on the floor. A damp towel hung over the towel rack, but it had partially dried. So, she hadn't used the towel recently, but had used it sometime after he'd left town.

Back in the bedroom, he noted the large blue bed cover which was usually on the bed was missing. He'd check the laundry just in case, but he suspected the bed covering was gone.

Ted headed for the stairs. "Come on, Ginger, let's look for Marcie."

Ace waited at the bottom of the stairs, like a good boy, wagging his tail.

He would have waited there, as he was trained, until Ted told him to come on up.

Ginger seemed to have had no training at all, but she was still a good little dog, given that she'd likely been pampered.

Heading outside, he let Ginger and Ace come with him.

He began to walk all around the house, looking at the ground for footprints.

Unfortunately, it had snowed recently which likely covered up any tracks an intruder would have left.

He suddenly felt like he was wasting time and needed to call the police and let the experts look the house over.

Ginger started sniffing around and he followed her, as she led him to the back yard. She ran toward a tree at the edge of the yard, and he followed her over to it.

Then she stopped, sniffed the ground, growled at a branch on the ground, and then barked several times, as if she was trying to tell him something.

"What did you find?" Ted asked.

He bent to look at the branch and then moved it aside. Beneath the branch, he saw a footprint on the ground. It looked like it had been made by a man's boot.

"Good girl," he said. "That footprint is too large to be Marcie's. Someone was out here. The snowstorm must have knocked this branch down. This is a lucky thing for us."

Ginger barked as if confirming yes, someone had been there, and yes, this was lucky.

"I wish you could tell me where she is and what's going on," he said. "I know you're trying. Okay, let's go back inside and wait for the police."

He took the little dog back inside, checked her water and food bowls which were empty. He filled both bowls and looked around the room.

Nothing appeared amiss in the kitchen.

He went and replaced the key exactly where he had found it.

Now that Ginger had food and water, he pulled out a kitchen chair, sat, and dialed 911.

"I would like to report a missing person," he said. "My girlfriend, Marcie. I had you do a drive-by to check on her. She's missing. I'm home from my trip and she didn't feed or water my dog or let him out. Then I came over to check on the little dog she's been dog-sitting and it's the same thing over here. Also, her purse and phone are still here."

"We have a car in the area, about ten minutes away," the dispatcher said.

That was good for the Poconos, where there were only so many patrol cars and houses were built in remote areas.

"Thanks," he said. When he hung up, he made another circle around the house, trying to see if there was any other way to get inside, other than the key being under the mat.

He paced, waiting for the police to arrive.

Ten minutes seemed to take forever.

When the patrol car pulled up and parked, two officers got out. A man and a woman.

"I'm glad you're here," Ted said. "My girlfriend is missing."

The policewoman held her hand up. "Slow down. Let's start at the beginning." She let her hand drop and pulled out a pad and pen to write with. "I'm officer Riley Wittman and this is officer Jimmy Schmitt. And you are?"

"Ted Barr," he said. "And my girlfriend's name is Marcie Hayes. I called in a safety check to you guys earlier, when I first realized she might be missing."

She nodded.

Officer Schmitt said, "We have that on record. No one answered the door and there was a dog inside, barking."

"I was hoping you would do more," Ted said.

"It's not against the law to go missing," Officer Schmitt said.

"Right," Ted said. "They told me that after I called the first time." He shook his head. "But nothing about Marcie's disappearance makes sense."

He gestured toward the house. "She left a dog inside who hadn't been fed, watered, or let out. You'll see the puddle by the door. It's the same with my dog, Ace, who she was supposed to be checking on while I was out of town at my brother's wedding. Marcie has vanished but Ginger is still here and neither dog had been taken care of when I got back home. Marcie would never do that. She's a dog lover."

"And where is home?" Officer Wittman asked.

He rattled off the address and then pointed. "Just down the street. That's how me met, walking the dogs. Then we started going out. I asked her to watch Ace while I went to my brother's wedding in Montana, last weekend, and I just arrived home an hour ago."

Officer Wittman frowned and glanced at Officer Schmitt. "Animal Control told me the pound is full. There's a foster list, but few takers." She glanced back to Ted.

"I'll take care of them both," he said. "Until Marcie is found."

She nodded, and seemed relieved that the dog situation was taken care of. Immediately she switched back into stern cop mode.

"Her full name," Officer Wittman said. "And any nick-names or aliases?" She waited, with her pen ready to write them down.

"Marcie Hayes," he said. "I don't know about nicknames or anything like that."

She nodded. They already had Marcie's full name. "Physical description."

"Blonde, five foot five, I don't know her weight, but she's curvy." He opened his phone. "I can show you a couple pictures of her."

"If you can provide three recent photos that would help," she said.

"I have three," he said as he showed them to her. "And there's more in her cell phone."

"She left her phone?" Officer Schmitt said. "That doesn't sound good."

Office Wittman gave her partner a quick exasperated look and then returned to asking questions. "What clothing and shoes was she last seen wearing?"

"I have no idea. I was out of town and the last time I saw her was the morning I flew out. She was wearing navy sweatpants and a white sweatshirt. Gray-and-pink slippers. But she likely changed clothes since then. She was still answering her phone for a while. Then she stopped."

"Does she wear glasses of contacts?"

"No," he said.

"Would she be carrying a purse, a wallet, or anything else?"

"Her purse is inside, too."

Officer Schmitt frowned.

Ted glanced at him. He agreed with what Officer Schmitt had said earlier. This did not sound good. It was clear to Ted that someone had taken her. He just needed the police to take this seriously and find her, soon.

"Does she have any scars, tattoos, or other identifying characteristics?"

"No scars or tattoos," he said.

"Allergies, disabilities, or other medical conditions?"

"I don't know." He shook his head. "We haven't been dating long. We just met at the beginning of December."

"Can you provide a list of relatives or close friends?"

"No family still living. Friends, I have no idea," he said. "All that information should be in her cell phone."

"How about a list of places she frequents?"

"She hasn't even been here a month, and I'd guess that the local grocery store is about the only place she's gone by herself," he said.

"Where might she have gone with someone else?" Officer Wittman asked.

I took her skiing and to dinner a couple of times in Scranton," he said.

Ted pointed to the vehicle sitting in the drive. "That's the loaner car that comes with the house. So, I doubt she drove off somewhere. There aren't any other cars for her to use."

Officer Wittman appeared done with her questioning, as she wrote the last part down.

Ted wished he had more information to give her, but the truth was, he and Marcie were still getting to know each other.

"How did you get inside the house?" Officer Wittman asked.

"The spare key," he said. "I unlocked the door and went in looking for Ginger, the little dog she is watching. Ginger was shut up in the bathroom with the door closed. Someone had to have put her in there. Marcie wouldn't have done that. She has a crate and Marcie would have put her in there if she were leaving."

"Take us through the house, retracing your steps," Officer Schmitt said. "And tell us if you touched anything."

"Okay," Ted turned, and they followed him inside.

Rather than trying to explain about the elf, when they got to the kitchen, Ted pointed to the list and said, "Beverly, the homeowner, had Marcie doing all kinds of crazy things for this elf contest, and she'd get her nose bent out of shape if Marcie didn't do things exactly as instructed. She was sending texts in all caps and blowing up Marcie's phone."

"Beverly's last name?" Officer Wittman asked.

"I don't know it," Ted said. "Marcie just called her Beverly."

"We can find that out easy enough," Officer Schwartz

said.

"She'll be listed if she is the property owner," Officer Wittman said.

"It's her house," Ted said. "She's also got a boyfriend named Zeke, but I don't have his last name either."

"We'll figure it out," Officer Schwartz said.

He knew that mentioning her crazy behavior would likely put Beverly on a person of interest list, but right now, he didn't care.

The woman had been losing it over an elf doll, which was not exactly a sane and normal reaction. And she hadn't been nice to Marcie, who was one of the sweetest women he had met.

Officer Wittman and Officer Schmitt both read the list, and she raised an eyebrow and gave her partner a look.

It reminded Ted of how he and his brother would communicate silently, with a look.

He wished he could talk to Jack right now.

They kept moving through the house, Officer Wittman making notes.

"No forced entry on the ground floor," Officer Schmitt said. They had gone through the first floor and then down into the basement. Everything was locked up tight.

"There's a key under the front mat," Ted said. "I told her not to leave it there, but to take it and put it back before the homeowner returned. I told her it wasn't safe to keep it there and thought she had followed my advice, because I put it on her key ring myself. She must have taken it off."

"The key is there now?" Officer Schmitt asked.

"Yes," Ted said. "I looked under the mat and then left it there." His prints would be on the key, but he'd just told them he'd handled that key. "I wish she had listened to me and kept it on her key ring."

Anyone breaking in might have found that key and let himself in.

Officer Schmitt went out to look for himself while Officer Wittman followed Ted upstairs. "It looks like she took a bubble bath as some point," he said. "There's still a damp towel in the bathroom."

They walked into her bedroom first.

Officer Wittman stopped short at the sight of the elf, which sat on the dresser, appearing to watch them.

"That," she said, "is not the kind of elf I was expecting."

"Ugly thing, isn't it?" Ted said. "Ginger hates it, and Marcie thinks it's creepy too. She hides it in the closet when she doesn't have to take pictures of it."

Officer Wittman frowned and looked from the doll to the bed and then back again. "It's positioned to watch the bed," she said.

"Exactly," Ted said. "And Marcie found that doll too creepy to ever have placed it there."

Frowning deeper, Officer Wittman stepped into the bathroom.

Ted stared at the elf and then followed the policeman, pointing things out he had noticed.

She finished making her notes and then came back out and looked closer at the doll. "Have you picked it up or touched it in any way?" she asked.

"Only when I helped her take pictures," he said. "So, my prints will be on it. I spent time here with her, so my prints are probably all through the house."

She nodded as if that were a given and pulled out her fingerprinting kit. "I'm going to start with this elf, because there are some things I want to look at," she said. "The rest can wait."

"Don't you have to wait for CSI?" he asked.

She gave him a look which said, really? "Jimmy and I are cook, bottle-washer, and waitress in this serve 'em up joint," she said. "Which makes us the local CSI here."

By now, she had her gloves on, the can of fingerprint powder open, and a brush ready to go. After dusting the doll, she took tape and got the cleanest prints that she could. Once she was done with that, she picked the doll up and looked closer at its face.

"Notice anything about the eyes on her?" she asked.

"No, but Marcie thought they could move and would watch her," Ted said.

She poked at the doll's eyes. "These aren't the original eyes," she said. "They've been replaced." She turned the doll over. "See this seam?"

He nodded.

"That's where the doll was stitched up, not so long ago," she said. "This seam is where they sewed her up again."

"How do you know so much about the doll?" Officer Schmitt asked.

"My grandmother used to repair old dolls," Officer Wittman said. "Her sister ran an antique shop and some of the dolls that came in were really messed up."

"Huh," Officer Schmitt said. He had come back up the stairs and was moving through the rooms, seeing what Officer Wittman had written down and what Ted had shown her.

Officer Wittman poked at one of the eyes on the doll and something moved inside. She felt the doll's body. "There's something inside her that doesn't belong," she said.

Taking out a bigger bag, she dropped the doll into it. "And if Marcie Hayes didn't like this doll, there's no way she would want it facing her when she was in bed."

"There's one more thing," Ted said.

Both officers looked at him.

"I found one footprint in the back yard near a tree," he said. "A fallen branch kept the snow from filling it in. It looks like a man's boot, too big to be one of Marcie's footprints."

"And you said a woman owns this house," Officer Wittman said. "No husband?"

"House always looks vacant when we drive past," Officer Schmitt said. "She must not come here much."

"Just a boyfriend," Ted said. "No husband. I don't know anything about how often she comes here."

"And where are they now?" Officer Wittman asked.

"In Miami for the holidays," he said. "That's why Marcie is house- and dog-sitting."

Officer Wittman made more notes, and then they all headed out to the back yard to look at the print he had found; the dogs happily running alongside and playing together.

Ted would have put them both up, but that hardly seemed fair as they had been cooped up and neglected while he was gone. Letting them run and play was good for them, and they weren't getting in anyone's way.

The officers did not seem to mind, and Ted suspected that Officer Wittman had a soft spot for dogs from the way she had first established that both dogs would be taken care of. An easy enough thing to do.

Maybe it was because they lived in a village, or a township, and the police force was small, but Ted noted this was not going at all like the shows on TV where the police wanted everyone to move out of the way and shut up.

They both were listening to him and letting him show them things. And they were taking him seriously about Marcie being missing.

The footprint in the wooded area behind the house needed to be investigated more fully. Freshly fallen snow would have made that more difficult.

Wind whipping through the trees swirled the snow about. Likely what had uncovered the one footprint he'd seen.

They started to make a circle around the footprint as they looked for more. Then started looking again, making the next circle wider.

They followed that pattern, making wider and wider circles looking for another footprint.

He glanced back toward the house and saw how far they'd gone. Whoever had been walking behind the house had walked a long way.

That was alarming to Ted.

He continued the pattern from before, hoping to finding more prints. But his luck had run out. Too much snow had fallen, covering the booted man's tracks.

She hadn't driven anywhere. The vehicle sat outside the house, the keys were inside, and she would have taken her purse if she had gone anywhere voluntarily.

Both officers had put their heads together and were conferring. Then Officer Wittman came back over to him. "We're going to put out a missing person on Marcie," she said. "We'll need those three photos you have of her."

"These are from when we went skiing," he said. "And her phone will have all those elf photos in it. She is in some of them and without all the bundled-up ski clothes. Plus, every text that crazy homeowner has sent her, yelling via text."

Officer Wittman nodded. "We'll be looking into all of that," she said. "Thank you for your help and cooperation."

"Thank you for believing me," he said. "And for listening."

"You're welcome," she said. "Are you going to take the little dog with you?"

"Yes," he said. "Let me grab her food and bowls along with a toy or two."

"Take her crate," Officer Wittman said. "That's always their safe space. Their home."

"You know dogs," he said.

"Yes," she said. "I had a K-9 when I worked in Boston. Ali." She smiled. "Great dog. Belgian Malinois. Got shot in the line of duty." She looked off into the trees. "I moved here after, thinking quiet village, less crime. Didn't need another K-9." Her eyes got misty, then she blinked the tears away and turned serious again.

"Criminals are everywhere," she said. "Just as mobile as anyone else." She shook her head. "You'd be surprised the amount of illegal activity taking place in small-town America."

"I'll bet," he said. "It's remote here. She might have been safer house-sitting in a city."

"Maybe, maybe not," Officer Wittman shrugged. "Criminals are everywhere."

"Find her," Ted said. "I'll do anything I can to help, but please, find her soon. Before something bad happens to her. Something worse than being taken."

Officer Wittman nodded.

Ted went into the house to get Ginger's things.

When he came out and put them and both dogs in his car, Officer Wittman was on her radio, talking to the sheriff's department and it sounded like the sheriff was on his way.

Ted drove home.

Officer Wittman had promised to call with an update later, and he had her business card with her name and number on it.

CHAPTER 11

The next morning, Marcie was still missing, and Ted was becoming impatient. He couldn't help that. He wanted Marcie found, safe, back where she belonged.

"Do you need to go out?" he asked the dogs.

Ginger barked excitedly and Ace woofed once.

"Okay, let me get your leashes and we'll go out." He would take care of the dogs, but he also needed to find Marcie.

"I wish you could tell me where she is and what's going on," he said to the little King Charles Spaniel, who wagged her tail and looked up at him.

His cell phone rang.

Officer Wittman.

"Hello?" he said.

"Ted, Officer Wittman here," she said.

"You found her?" He couldn't hold back from asking.

"Not yet," she said. "But we did find a camera in that elf doll."

What in the hell was going on?

Anger ran through his entire body.

"Some son of a bitch has been filming her?"

"Looks like it," she said.

"Dammit." His hand clenched into a fist. He wanted to seriously hurt whoever was behind that camera. "I want that creep put away, and Marcie found."

"The good news is," Officer Wittman went on, "this changes the MO and escalates the case from a missing person to a serious kidnapping."

"That's good news?" He couldn't help reacting emotionally.

This was Marcie. Kidnapping was not good news, dammit.

"It's good news because this means we can now call in the state police," Officer Wittman explained. "State crime scene techs are headed to the house now to do a secondary search and collect evidence. There's a higher chance of finding her, with their help."

"Tell me what you know or suspect," Ted said, now controlling his rage.

This was not the time to explode. That would not help them find Marcie.

"We've got a voyeur," she said. "Guy who likes to watch. Stalker-type. He's probably been watching since she first saw that elf when she got to the house. Tell me more about the elf."

"It was here when she arrived," Ted said. "The homeowner wanted Marcie to read that set of instructions before she even greeted the dog and let her out. The woman is obsessed with winning that contest. There's something wrong with this whole situation."

"She could be connected with Marcie's disappearance," Officer Wittman said. "Whether she knew about the camera or not, it's her doll. We're running background checks on

Beverly and on the boyfriend, Zeke. Have you ever met either of them?"

"No," Ted said. "Marcie doesn't really know them either. She's only talked to Beverly by phone or text. Zeke claims to have met her after she house-sat for his cousin, but she didn't remember him when he called out of the blue to schedule her to house sit for Beverly."

"So, the arrangements for this job were done over the phone," Officer Wittman said. "Does Marcie do anything to vet the people she works for?"

"I have no idea," he said. That was something they would be talking about when she was safely back. That, and other things relating to her safety. Right now, they had to get her back. "How long will it take the state police to start looking for her?" he asked.

"That will depend on what the state crime scene techs find," she said.

ZEKE STARED AT THE VIDEO, livid, as he watched the tall man looking at the elf.

From inside Marcie's bedroom!

Where he was standing in front of the elf.

He knows Marcie by name.

Rage ran through Zeke, and he narrowed his eyes as he watched the man moving.

Who the hell is he, and why is he in Marcie's bedroom? How did he get in? Did he know about the key under the doormat? Has he been in there before?

He turned and ran down the stairs to the basement, glaring at the blonde who lay sleeping on the bed, her arms and legs tied to the corners, a red-and-white see-through nightie the only thing she wore.

He'd set her up this way to take pictures, earlier. Video would come later.

After he tied her, he'd gone upstairs to watch the final videos taken of Marcie in the bathtub.

She was just as he'd left her.

She looks so innocent. My perfect Christmas present.

It was hard to believe she'd let some stranger into the house, and into her bed.

But the man was there, standing in front of the elf, talking to it.

So, who is this guy? Had she let him see her naked? Given herself to him?

She was his perfect Christmas gift. She couldn't belong to anyone else.

But if she had a boyfriend that no one knew about ... and if that boyfriend visited her when she was house-sitting ...

Then maybe Marcie wasn't the sweet and innocent girl that she seemed to be.

The fact had stared him in the face, literally, as the man looked at the elf. The man was in that room, knew her name, and now knew she was missing.

This raised an element of danger for Zeke that hadn't been there before.

He would not get caught. He'd make sure of that. He never got caught with anything. Not since he was a little boy. His mother had taken those secrets to her grave.

He flicked on the overhead lights, which now brightened up the basement room showing him everything in every corner. There was no hiding beneath these lights.

She woke, blinked, then closed her eyes against the brightness.

"Who the hell is he?" he shouted at her.

She frowned, as if she didn't know what he was talking about.

"The man in your bedroom," he clarified, waiting for her answer.

Her expression did not change as she turned her gaze up to the ceiling to avoid looking at him. Which meant she was trying to avoid answering. She had to know who the man was.

"Who is he?" he demanded again.

"I don't know. I'm clearly *not* in my bedroom, now" she retorted, her gaze returning to him. "*You* took me, so *you* figure it out."

That saucy little mouth of hers was going to get her into trouble.

He could shut her up by stuffing something into it.

But not now. Not when he wanted answers.

"Tall guy. Thin. Dark hair. Tell me who he is," he said. "And why he knows your name."

She smirked. "I'll give you his name, when you give me yours."

He circled the bed, watching her.

Defiant little doll, he thought, not for the first time. *Thinks she's so smart.*

Even if she were smart, he was smarter. She would never outthink him.

Few women had ever come close. People were so easily fooled once you knew how.

She was certainly more defiant than he'd imagined her to be before he took her. He'd seen early signs of her independent streak when she couldn't follow the elf rules exactly as they were laid out for her. Had to start doing things her way. Ruining the plans that he and Beverly had made for her to follow.

It hadn't taken much to make Beverly angry about it. Growing up with servants who did what they were told had spoiled her, and now she expected anyone she hired to do exactly as they were told, no exceptions, because Beverly had said so.

A defiant girl, like Marcie, would have been sacked, early on.

Beverly was close to doing just that when he had intervened and reminded her that the girl would be gone after the holidays and Beverly would never have to deal with her again.

Since Beverly liked to be in charge, or think she was, he always had to make her think that an idea was hers, not his, and then she would go along with it. She would run his life if he'd let her. Probably thought that once they were married, she would.

But that was never going to happen.

He'd found a perverse pleasure in seeing his girlfriend chew out his side girl, while she remained unaware of the real reason Marcie had been hired.

Those pretty lips of hers for one. Her breasts for another. Her pretty face and figure and, most of all, the fact that no one would know if she went missing.

That part of the plan was now all blown to hell.

Now, this man Zeke had not known about knew, and it was clear that he missed Marcie.

She was both defiant and secretive. What a naughty girl.

He would come up with a punishment.

As he walked around the bed, over and over, pacing, she watched him out of the corners of her eyes.

He paced like the big cats in the zoo, hoping to see even a little fear in her eyes.

But it wasn't there.

She wanted a name. He would indulge her and give her one, to see what her reaction would be.

He stopped abruptly and faced her. "Simon," he said. "Now it's your turn. His name."

"Simon," she repeated. "Simon, please let me go."

"Oh no," he said. "Simon says that won't do. I gave you a name and now you must give me one. Tell me his name."

"Ted," she said.

"Ted what? What's his last name?"

"What's yours?" Her eyes were sharp, watching him.

He knew she didn't believe he would give her a last name, so he simply smiled.

Leaving her, he went back up the stairs, suddenly realizing she was going to be the most difficult of the four women he had taken so far.

Though he didn't want to start the injections so soon, he might have no choice.

She would never be compliant without them.

He'd done the chloroform just right this time, unlike the first time when the woman who'd inhaled too much as he'd held it over her nose, pressing down, had struggled.

She hadn't lasted long.

How was he supposed to know that holding it over her nose longer than five minutes might kill her?

The damn woman wouldn't quit kicking and trying to fight. Until all the fight was gone.

She'd been the most disappointing of the four, as he hadn't gotten to play with her at all. As a result, he had no pictures, no videos, nothing for him to watch.

She died too soon. Such a waste.

But never mind that.

He was more experienced now and knew what to do to keep this one alive, a long time.

Taking out the medical supplies, he filled a syringe and carried it downstairs.

He didn't speak to her as he approached.

Suddenly, he jabbed the needle into her left arm, enjoying her reaction as he injected the drug.

Her eyes, wide with terror, watched him, but she remained silent.

She could see the room was soundproofed, so she knew screaming wouldn't bring anyone to save her.

She'd tried that at first, until her throat became hoarse, and she'd needed water.

Zeke watched as her eyes took on a glazed look, which told him the drug was working.

He went back upstairs to finish watching the footage from the camera in the elf.

Calming himself down, to pay attention to any details he might see on the video, he watched it until the end.

Until what he saw before the video shut off made him worry for the first time in many years.

A lady cop bent down to look at the elf more closely and was saying that something about the elf was wrong.

She'll probe until she finds the camera. She has that look about her.

He just knew she would.

Women cops were the worst because they had to earn their place working beside the men. It made them tougher because they thought they had more to prove. Which they did. Most had tenacity and persistence which went above and beyond.

He knew what would come next.

There would be a missing person's report. Then Beverly would know the house-sitter was missing.

The worry about being caught crossed his mind. He would have to be very careful.

The way I bought that camera, no one will trace it to me. And I put it in the elf myself.

The elf though. It's traceable back to that antique shop and the doll repair place. Which comes right back to me.

His mind raced for a moment and then, with his usual clarity, he thought again.

It's not against the law to buy an old elf as a gift.

He glanced at the bookshelves which held research materials he could not keep at home.

Nor is it against the law to go missing.

He was certain the police would question him. He could be tied to the house-sitter, but so could his cousin. And he could be tied to the elf.

Neither of those facts would send him to jail.

Police needed hard evidence, like DNA and computer records. He'd make sure they would have neither.

He would practice what he would say to the police and practice it often enough that it would be as natural as any thought that popped into someone's head.

Quietly, he rehearsed what he would tell the police when they questioned him.

"How was I supposed to know the girl would be so unreliable?" he would say. "My cousin told me she had done a great job for him. That's why we hired her."

Beverly was paying for the house-sitting, so it was important to present a united front of 'we.'

He was sure his girlfriend would be naturally upset with the girl, her reactions genuine enough not to be seen as faked.

He would tell them he sent the doll out to have new stuffing put into it and to be cleaned so it wouldn't smell as Beverly can't abide smelly antiques.

She was sure to confirm that statement.

He'd tell them: "Here's where I bought the elf and here's the doll repair people's contact information; you can ask them about what all they did to it. How am I supposed to know what they put into that doll? I paid for new stuffing, that's all I asked them to do." He would pretend to look in his phone for their information and jot it down.

"Here you go, Officer," he would say, holding the piece of paper out. "Let me know if there is anything else I can do to help."

That would be easy. All truths and not one lie to have to remember. That was always the best way.

There was a reason he hadn't been caught since he was a boy. He'd learned to be smarter. He gave the police procedures book a grin.

You just had to be smarter than the police.

With his IQ being, as his grandfather had said, 'off the charts,' that wasn't hard for Zeke.

The old man had wanted to get him into some special third-grade class for smart kids, before he'd keeled over in his fishing boat from a heart attack.

He was the only relative Zeke missed. The only one who had cared that Zeke was bored out of his mind in school.

By fourth grade, Zeke was getting into trouble at school, out of sheer boredom.

By fifth grade, he was running around with older kids that his grandfather would never have approved of, and was learning things he would have been paddled for doing, if he'd ever been caught.

When his mother had married a second, wealthier

husband, and shipped Zeke off to boarding school in sixth grade, he began to acquire his polish. He put aside the wilder stuff, learning that money and good manners would get him what he wanted much easier.

Now he was a respectable businessman, working in Manhattan, with a wealthy, social girlfriend, and they would both clearly be shocked that the girl had gone missing.

Because that was what decent society people would do, and he had an image to maintain.

He'd sent the elf out to be worked on, to make it the perfect gift for Beverly. How could he have known it would come back with a camera in it?

That was his story, and he was sticking with it.

This situation could still be salvaged if it went that far.

If it did, the cops would reach a dead end. He'd see to that.

No victim, no crime. They'll have to find her first.

A lot of people go missing every single day. Marcie would be just one more on that list. She's my little secret, and I am going to keep her that way.

He switched the video from the police officer to the earlier taping of where Marcie was undressing for the bubble bath. He pushed further thoughts of the police-woman aside for the rest of the night. Once he'd watched Marcie in the bath enough times, he would go downstairs and play with her further.

Video of her in that Santa's helper costume would be first.

~

TED WAS NOT CONVINCED the police were doing enough to find Marcie. And even if they were, they had other calls to go on, so he was not going to count on them to find her.

Picking up the phone, he called his buddy, Nathan. It was time to call in his network of friends who knew how to get things done.

"Nathan," he said, when his friend picked up the phone. "I've got a situation here."

That was how he began the first of ten calls to his buddies.

Nathan volunteered to do flyovers in his private plane, whenever Ted said the word.

"Thanks, I'll let you know," Ted said.

Jack was the next call.

"Hey, Bro, I know you're on your honeymoon, but ..." he started off on his explanation for the interuption, but Jack interrupted him before he could finish.

"Is it Mom and Dad?" his anxious brother asked. "Are they okay?"

"Yeah, they're both fine, off on their cruise," Ted said. "But I have a situation out here."

"What's up?" his brother asked.

"I've got a new girlfriend," Ted said, and his brother interrupted again.

"That's great, Bro, but ya know ya could've waited till the honeymoon was over to tell me that," Jack said.

"No, I couldn't, because she's missing, and it looks like she's been taken."

"Damn. Give me the intel." Jack was serious now, his tone that of the Marine that he was.

"I tried calling her before I flew back home," Ted said. "Multiple times, no answer. Had the police drive by to do a welfare check and no Marcie, just the dog, barking in the house. But it's not against the law to go missing, so nothing else was done, until I got home and went over to the house. She hadn't fed, watered, or let out Ace or Ginger, the dog she's watching. Her purse is there and the car, but no trace of her. And then, there's the elf."

"Elf?" Jack asked. "What the hell, man? Is this a gag or prank?"

"I wish it was." Jack's voice held his frustration. "No, this is an elf doll, which the police discovered had a camera inside. Some demented son of a bitch has been watching her with it, and now she's gone."

Jack kept him on the phone longer, asking more questions.

Once Ted had told Jack all he knew, Jack said. "I'll put in a call to Hank Patterson at Brotherhood Protectors. See what contacts he has out your way and what resources we can bring in to help. A lot of people go missing in the U.S., Bro, but there are also many men who are good at finding them. Don't lose hope."

"We have to find her, Jack," Ted said. "The alternative is unthinkable."

"I'll call you back after I talk to Hank," Jack said.

A mumble in the background came from his new bride.

"No, baby," Jack told her. "I've got to make a couple important calls before we go out to dinner and then I'm all yours."

"Sorry to interrupt your honeymoon," Ted said.

"I would have been more upset if you hadn't called," Jack said, "when you know I can help. If you need to call me, don't hesitate."

"Thanks," Ted said, his voice choking the word out.

His twin was always there for him. Even on his honeymoon.

Things were serious when Ted had to interrupt his brother like that and now the emotion he'd tamped down started to leak out.

Marcie couldn't be gone. But she was.

He forced his emotions back down. He didn't have time for that.

"You never have to thank me, Bro," Jack said. "You gonna be okay?"

"Yeah," Ted forced out. "Call Hank."

"On it." And with a click, Jack hung up the phone.

Which was exactly what Ted needed him to do.

This wasn't the time to get emotional. Marcie was missing and they had to get her back before something terrible happened to her. They could not fail.

OFFICER WITTMAN KNOCKED on Ted's door. This time she was alone.

The dogs were barking when he opened the door.

"Flying solo today?" he asked.

"Office Schmitt is at the dentist today," she said. "So yes, I'm flying solo. How are the dogs doing?"

"Great, as you can see," he said. He reached into his pocket and gave them each a treat, which they both eagerly took.

They trotted off with their treats and he waved her inside. "Come on in," he said.

She stepped inside, and they followed the dogs over to the couch. She took a seat in the chair across from it and he sank down into the couch.

"I thought I'd stop by and update you on where things

stand," she said. "See if you remember anything else that might help us find Marcie."

"Good," he said. "Coffee?"

"Nothing for me," she said.

Glad to be done playing host to a guest in his home, he leaned back against the cushions. "What progress has been made?"

She flipped her notepad open and was ready with her pen.

"So, this elf contest, which I'd never heard of, apparently has a big following on social media," Officer Wittman started. "And a five-thousand-dollar prize, but even people who aren't trying to win seem to be obsessed with these elves. There are whole fan groups and that elf, which goes by the name of Tananna, has fans."

"You're kidding," Ted said.

"I'm serious, and so is this." She pointed to a printout which showed a picture of the elf. "We've been circulating this picture to see what we can learn about the elf, and we found the antique dealer who sold it. The bill of sale was to a Zeke R. Kingsley."

"We already knew Beverly's boyfriend had given her the elf, so I don't see how this helps to find Marcie," Ted said.

"The antique dealer emphasized that Mr. Kingsley had made a big deal about having the old stuffing removed and new stuffing put in. She didn't want him to do that because it's an antique and it would devalue the doll. But he insisted that Beverly had allergies and he could not give her the elf unless it was cleaned up."

Ted had a gut feeling about this guy. "So, he insisted, huh?"

"According to her." Officer Wittman nodded. "She's still

upset about giving him the name of a place that would do that doll surgery for him."

Doll surgery? To put that camera in. That damn elf.

Ted thought about all the times Marcie had said the elf made her feel uncomfortable and how Ginger would bark at it. He should have looked closer at the elf and paid more attention. Instead, he'd brushed off their reactions to the elf, thinking it a harmless doll.

That dog is smarter than any of us.

Often dogs knew things that people didn't.

Officer Wittman knew dogs. She would understand what he was about to tell her.

"So," Ted began, "I didn't think to tell you this earlier, but Ginger hates that elf. So much so, that every time Marcie brought the thing out, she would bark and growl at it. Marcie ended up putting it in a closet when she wasn't taking photos for that stupid contest."

"Smart dog," Officer Wittman said. "Assuming someone entered the house to take Marcie, how would they get past Ginger? If she barked at the stuffed elf, she surely would have barked at an intruder."

"Unless she knew the intruder," Ted said. "Unless it was the boyfriend."

"Zeke Kingsley is on the list," she said. "He just flew back to New York from Miami."

"I thought he was supposed to be spending the month of December down there with his girlfriend. What's he doing in New York?"

"His office is in Manhattan," she said. "Apparently he flies back and forth."

"Well, that's mighty convenient, since we're only two hours from New York City," he said. "Don't forget. Beverly didn't find Marcie and hire her. He's the one who suggested

Beverly hire her. So when are you going to bring him in?" In his frustration, he fired his last words at her.

She shot him a look. "I haven't forgotten a thing," she said, her sharp tone making it clear that she did not like his implication that she had. "And we will be questioning him." She cleared her throat and brought her tone back to a more neutral one. "Here's the part you're not going to like. As you know, we are a small police department. I've told the sheriff what's going on and he says we're going to have to wait for the state police to get here."

"You're right," he said. "I don't like hearing that. The clock is ticking. Every minute, every hour that goes by, is another hour she is missing."

"I hate that, too," she said. "When I worked in the city, we had CSI, and detectives, and hundreds of officers. Everything moves slow on this mountain."

"Too damn slow." He shook his head. "I can't wait on you and your partner to figure things out. I've called in some help. Guys who know how to find people. I hope you don't have a problem with that and will work with them. We need to find her sooner, not later."

She gave him an intense look for a moment, and then said, "Finding her is my top priority unless I get sent out on a call. So, I don't have a problem with that, if your guys can work with us and not hinder us in finding her."

"Oh, that's no problem at all," he said. "Some of these guys can be in and out of an area without you even knowing they'd been there."

"This isn't a military OP," she said. "It's not a matter of getting her out. We must find her first. And that takes detective-type work, not muscles and guns."

"So, what else do you know about this Zeke guy?" he asked. "Dig up anything?"

"He's got a squeaky-clean background," she said.

Already that made Ted suspiscious.

"Fancy boarding schools, expensive college, high-dollar job in Manhattan with a high-dollar apartment there. No other houses to stash her in. And she's not in Beverly's, which is the only home she owns. Beverly stays at her parents' house often. Plenty of servants there to wait on her hand and foot. She's never held a job. Her daddy spoils her rotten."

"Could he hide Marcie in his Manhattan apartment?"

"Highly unlikely," she said. "The doorman said he's had no visitors for two years. No one goes up to Zeke's apartment other than himself and his cleaning lady." She stood to go.

"Oh, and that's not suspicious," Ted couldn't help the sarcasm. He stood. "He's a weirdo," Ted shook his head. "Probably watches tapes from stalking her in his 'nobody comes in here,'" he flashed his fingers to emphasize the words, "apartment."

"We'd need a search warrant to enter," she said.

"How do you get one from New York?" he asked.

"That's the other thing," Officer Wittman said. "We're dealing with three states here. It's not as easy as when everything is in the same town, but I will do all that I can." Frustration was evident in her voice. She moved toward the door, and he followed her. "I will keep following any lead we have," she said.

"My guys will be here tomorrow," he said. "They may have questions."

"Happy to answer them," she said.

"Will the FBI come in on this?" he asked.

"Maybe," she said.

"I don't want people fighting over whose job it is to do what," he said. "No pissing contests between agencies."

"It's not like on TV," she said. "We work together with a common goal."

"You've worked with the FBI, then?"

"I have. And ATF. And Homeland Security. And U.S. Marshals."

"Wow," he said. For the first time, he was impressed. "You managed that, working in this little village?"

"No. I was a city cop for several years. Till my dog got shot." She sniffed and he almost offered her a tissue. But then she toughened up again, right before his eyes. "We've got a search dog coming with the state police."

"My guys are bringing a couple with them," he said.

"Thought you didn't want a pissing contest," she said.

"I don't."

"Then don't start one," she said. "When the state crime scene techs finish processing the scene, then your guys can take a look around and start a search."

He gave her a salute.

Her radio crackled to life as she headed toward her patrol car.

"Stay safe out there," he called.

She raised her hand in acknowledgement and then got in her car.

He watched her go, thinking how she was the first female cop he'd known, and he'd taken a liking to her. She'd be a good friend to have. A straight shooter. Once Marcie was back, he wanted them to meet. Females needed other females to talk to, and he'd wondered at Marcie's lack of friends. She'd said she moved around too much to make friends everywhere she went so she didn't bother anymore.

Where are you, Marcie?

The search dogs could not get here fast enough.

He walked over to Beverly's house and saw a crime scene

tech in the back yard beneath the tree where he'd found the boot print, while others were walking into the house carrying bags with their equipment.

"I'm the one who found that," he called out.

"Ted Barr?" One of the crime scene techs with a clipboard called out his name.

"That's me," Ted called back.

The man nodded, and moved closer so he didn't have to yell. "We're going to need a hair sample."

"Okay," Ted said. He'd already given the Gouldsboro police his fingerprints.

He stood still while the tech obtained a hair sample from him and then put it into a plastic bag. Then he turned back to the tech who squatted down, working beneath the tree.

"How will you get a print from that boot print?" he asked. "The snow has made it pretty wet back there."

The man working on the boot print said, "I'll show you how we do it."

"Thanks," Ted said.

"We recover shoe prints using casting," the man said. "Plaster of Paris."

Ted watched as the man first cleared away leaves and pebbles from the print. Then he sprayed hairspray across it.

While he waited for that to dry, he put two parts plaster mix to one part water in a plastic bag and mixed it up.

Once that was ready, he poured the plaster of Paris in one end of the print and allowed it to slowly fill up the indentation.

"It has to dry overnight," the man said. "But once it's removed, it can be used to compare with one of the suspect's boots."

"Do we have a solid suspect?" Ted asked.

"Solid doesn't happen until we have enough evidence," Officer Wittman spoke from behind him.

He hadn't heard her approach and jumped.

"Trace evidence has been found on the damp towel in the bathroom," she said. "A piece of hair was found on the bath towel, and it doesn't appear to be Marcie's. The crime scene tech found a brush with hairs in it and those hairs look different than the one on the towel. The towel and the hairbrush have been collected as evidence and are being sent to the crime lab for comparison."

"So that's why you guys wanted a sample of my hair," he said.

The crime scene tech stood and nodded.

"This is how we build a case," Officer Wittman said. "Piece by piece until it all comes together into a grouping of evidence. And the more we have, the better."

Ted headed back home to take Ace for a walk. He couldn't stand just sitting around waiting when he should be looking for Marcie. He needed to stay busy until the team got there.

MARCIE HAD SPENT SO much time sleeping that every time she woke, she went through wondering where she was again before her eyes adjusted and she remembered.

She dreamed the strangest dreams of dancing elves who laughed at her and a little dog who would not stop barking.

At a certain point, she realized she had been drugged. All this sleep was not natural for her, and strange dreams weren't, either.

He dressed and undressed her as if she were a doll and took all manner of photos of her. He gave her a sponge bath and then rubbed lotion and powder on her in various places, while she kept her eyes closed. He knew she was awake, but he didn't seem to mind her keeping them closed while he did all these things.

It was as if she didn't have to be inside her body for him to enjoy playing with it. So, mentally, she tried not to be.

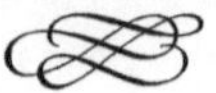

CHAPTER 12

The team had arrived with two K-9s and eight men. His brother's call to Hank Patterson had turned out five Brotherhood Protectors to help.

Ricky "Rock" Trumbull and his German Shepard K-9 Hercules, both former Delta Force; Sergeant Tim "Timbers" Watson Marine vet; Barrett Williams Green Beret vet; Brian "Barbie" Ken Marine Force Recon vet had all flown out from Montana to help him.

From the east coast, four SEALs had joined the team, thanks to Brotherhood Protector and SEAL vet Travis "Ballistic" Bannerman; active-duty SEAL Tanner "Diesel" Taylor; active-duty SEAL Tony "Cutter" Cuttino; the last K-9 handler, active-duty SEAL Sawyer "Pipes" Ferguson, and his German Shepherd K-9 Rambone.

The guys he hadn't met yet introduced themselves.

This job wasn't an official Brotherhood Protectors job, and Hank wanted to keep the company name low-profile this time, so they'd agreed to call themselves Ted's Team for this mission.

It gave him a lump in his throat, knowing that all these

men had dropped everything to come here and help him find his missing girlfriend.

Now that the state crime scene techs had done a secondary search, protected the crime scene and collected evidence, Officer Wittman said it would be okay for the team to wander around and look for things. She'd become enthusiastic once she heard they'd be bringing two K-9s trained in search and rescue.

State police could bring in a K9s, but the Gouldsboro police department was too small and not well enough funded to invest in bringing a trained K9 onto their police force.

The plan was to let the dogs from Ted's Team sniff Marcie's clothes and then start searching from the ground around the house to the tree where the footprint had been, in the hope that one of the dogs would pick up a trail that would lead to her.

"I appreciate your help," he told the team. "This is outside my skillset," Ted said. "I just fly fighter jets. First time in my life I've ever wished I was a PJ, with some search and rescue experience under my belt."

"You're good, man," Diesel said. "We got you covered."

Bedrolls were set up all throughout Ted's house and the dogs were introduced.

Ginger was chasing her tail in circles; she was so excited. But neither of the two K-9s cared about that. They both just laid down, resting their heads on their front paws, and watched her.

"Silly dog," Ted said. "I'll have to put you in your crate if you don't settle down. These guys need to rest because we start early tomorrow."

They ended up crating all four dogs because the K-9's owners said that all the dogs needed a good night's sleep.

Ace could be a night owl and would prowl the rooms of the house before he would go to sleep each night. Usually, Ted left the door to his crate open but tonight, he made sure they were all closed so no dogs would be roaming the house.

EARLY THE NEXT MORNING, they started out. He took the men and the dogs over to Beverly's house in two trips in his Blazer, because there were so many of them.

The dogs sniffed all around the front yard and then peed, marking territory.

Ted brought out Marcie's jeans and a pair of her socks for the dogs to sniff.

He hoped that Marcie's scent hadn't faded too much for them to track her.

Walking a grid behind her house in wider and wider circles had turned up nothing.

But these were dogs who found living people or bodies under piles of rubble. Ace and Ginger were not trained to sniff and to hunt like these dogs had been trained.

Rambone and Hercules stopped, to sniff around the tree where Ginger had helped Ted discover the boot print. But that didn't last long. Then they were off, sniffing, going back through the woods.

The men followed in a fan formation, to cover all the possible ground she might have gone through or been taken through.

Hercules caught the scent first and then he was off, Rambone running along beside him.

At last, they were on the trail of something.

Ted hoped like hell it wasn't a deer.

They ran a long way and then stopped, near a road, and

sniffed around in a circle on the road. The dogs sat, as if the job was done.

"That's it?" Ted asked.

"When they're done, they're done," Ricky "Rock" Trumbull said, as he reached into his pocket to retrieve a treat for his dog, Hercules.

Sawyer "Pipes" Ferguson got a treat out for his K-9 Rambone as well. "The trail ends here. They dinna stop, till it does."

"Likely he brought her through the woods and then put her in a vehicle for his getaway," Barrett Williams said.

"Great," Ted said. "Now what?"

"We go back to the house and regroup," Travis "Ballistic" Bannerman said.

THE WOMAN who had worked on the elf doll, unstuffing and restuffing it, had taken before, during, and after photos for her website. She was happy to provide the police with those photographs and claimed she had no idea how or why a camera would have been put inside of it.

"They would have had to take out a bunch of that good new stuffing I put in there," she said. "What a waste."

AFTER HAVING pizzas delivered and allowing the dogs to rest, Tony "Cutter" Cuttino went into Ted's back yard for a walk, to stretch his legs.

When he came back in, he asked Ted, "Have you checked your back yard out?"

"No," Ted said. "I haven't lived here long."

"You fly boys," Sergeant Tim "Timbers" Watson said. "If you can't do it from the air ..." He shook his head. "You have to check your ground perimeter, man."

"I just bought this house," Ted said, "And I haven't had a chance."

A few of the guys exchanged glances and Ted knew without any of them saying, that a perimeter check around the house was the first thing they would have done, the first night.

Truth was, Marcie had done a better job of that than Ted had.

But she'd still gone missing.

The team came up with a new plan, to check the perimeter of Ted's house, with the dogs, expanding out in a wider and wider circle.

It wasn't long until they found the camera.

"I didn't know there was a camera back here," Ted said. "I've been too busy setting up the house to do any exploring." He realized now that that had been a mistake.

If he'd known the camera was back there, the police could have had the footage right away. But at least he knew about it now.

"It's a hunting camera," Barrett Williams said. "For catching wild game. Too close to the house to be legal." He shook his head.

"The previous owner must have put it up and forgotten to mention it, because the realtor didn't say anything about it," Ted said.

"Not the homeowner," Travis "Ballistic" Bannerman shook his head. "Poachers. Unless your homeowner was one. They don't care about legal. Previous homeowner might not have known it was out there."

"I'd better call Officer Wittman," Ted said. "They'll want to know about this."

"Let's see if we can watch the footage first," Tony "Cutter" Cuttino said.

They all agreed that was a good idea.

As they watched the video footage, a van pulled up and parked on the side of the road.

A figure exited the van and then walked through the woods, wearing a face mask, and passed through the wooded area behind Ted's back yard.

"Look at the time and date," Sawyer "Piper" Ferguson said. "There's yer stalker."

"He's wearing a mask," Ted said.

Disappointment made his hopes drop again.

"Damn. I was hoping we'd get a face so we could try the facial recognition program we have access to," Brian Williams said.

The figure moved through the woods and past Ted's house, as they watched.

Nothing happened for a long time, until finally he was seen coming back through the woods toward the van, carrying something wrapped in a blanket-type of covering.

This time, he wasn't wearing a mask.

"You got your wish, Brian," Tanner "Diesel" Taylor said. "We can enhance that, and it looks like some clear shots of his face."

The figure carried his bundle all the way to the van, opened the side door, and placed the large bundle inside.

"Looks large enough to be a woman," Tony "Cutter" Cuttino said.

"Now the police can compare his face to their list of suspects," Ricky "Rock" Trumbull said. "They can pull photos from the DMV."

"Beverly's boyfriend is at the top of that list," Ted said.

"If that's him on the video, then we've got him," Barrett Williams said. "That's enough for the police to get an arrest warrant and a search warrant for his New York apartment."

"I'll call Officer Wittman right away," Ted said.

CHAPTER 13

The game camera video gave the police enough to get an arrest warrant for Zeke Kingsley, because they could identify Zeke from the video and a photo of his New York driver's license.

Internet searches had turned up enough about Zeke Kingsley, to learn he was a wealthy socialite associated with Beverly Westwood.

But they still didn't know where Marcie was and to Ted, that was what mattered most.

"Everything is taking too damn long," he said.

His team was gathered around him, inside his house, talking strategy for their next move.

"We've done the ground search, now we'll search by air," Barrett Williams said.

"Good," Ted said.

"We can use a drone or a helicopter with a thermal-imaging camera," Barrett added.

Sweeps of the area by helicopter began, with two men in the helicopter, while Ted waited on the ground.

"It found nothing near the house," Barrett said through the radio which was turned up so all the team could hear. "But it picked up a heat source several miles away. Will head that way to check it out."

Brian "Barbie" Ken had a topographic map spread out across the dining room table and was marking it as the helicopter searched an area. "Give me the coordinates of the heat source," he said, pen in hand.

Barrett called the coordinates in, and Brian marked it on the map.

"Getting closer," Barrett said. "Looks like a smoldering van just off the road."

"Can you land and check it out?" Ted asked.

"No. We have traffic," Barrett said. "Couple of semis. Heading back in to regroup. Police will want to know about the van."

"I'll call it in," Ted said.

At least making calls to Officer Wittman gave him something to do and she always updated him when he called.

Once the team was all back together again, Tanner "Diesel" Taylor said, "Okay, let's take the helicopter up again and this time do a search for areas around this van in the direction that he might have gone."

"Sounds like a solid plan," Barrett said after listening to the voicemail on his phone. "You go ahead. Hank called me for an update on our search and the situation report so I'll call him back."

THEY MOVED the search to an area around the smoldering van and made the search circle wider and wider and eventually found an old cabin back in the woods.

"The cabin has two heat sources inside, but we don't know who the heat sources belong to. Could be Marcie and her kidnapper, or it could be a couple on vacation."

Ted called Officer Wittman to give her the information right away.

"Your team guys need to wait for us to formulate a plan," she said. "Don't let them go rushing in there. If Marcie is in that cabin, that could get her killed."

"I understand," he said. The last thing he wanted anyone to do was to endanger Marcie more than she already might be.

After informing the police what they found, and confirming that the cabin could be a hideout, his team and the state and local police would all need to work together to check out the cabin and its interior.

Though Ted's Team had no police authority, they had better equipment to locate Marcie with, so the state and local police would allow them to help look for her and welcomed their help and better equipment.

Everyone just wanted Marcie found and the kidnapper put away for a long time.

***

After a joint meeting, the plan they agreed upon was, that Ted's Team, being good at stealthily moving into an area and out again, would help the local and state police surround the cabin. They would cut off the route away from the cabin, and be ready to catch him, if they could flush him out.

They needed Zeke to leave the cabin so the police could see him to know that it was him and not someone else.

The best scenario would be to arrest him away from the

cabin so he couldn't run back inside and create a nasty barricade situation, with Marcie in there.

A shootout could get her killed.

ONE OF TED'S TEAM, BRIAN "BARBIE" Ken, had already snuck up near the cabin and placed a GPS tracker on Zeke's car. If he made it past the Stop Sticks they put out for him, they would still be able to track him.

Ted's Team and the local and state police were waiting in the woods surrounding the cabin. Officer Matt Taylor with the state police, was also there with his canine partner, Lars.

Officer Wittman had seen Lars in action before, and hoped he got a chance to take a good juicy bite out of Zeke Kingsley, as he took the perp down.

Once everyone was in place and ready, Officer Wittman would call Beverly.

They had the one road leading out of the wooded area ready with a tire-deflation device. Their best chance to stop Zeke's vehicle.

Car chases could be dangerous for everyone involved, so the sooner they stopped his car, the better.

"How does that work?" Ted asked.

"The officers have thrown Stop Sticks across the road, setting them up with rope, ready to pull them across," Tanner "Diesel" Taylor said. He, like many of the other team members, was wearing a headset and could hear the police talking to each other. "He won't get a vehicle through there without flattening his tires."

Part of Ted's Team stayed behind to rescue Marcie, if they found out she was in the cabin tied up and unable to free herself. Their K9's had stayed behind, as they did not have the authority to arrest Zeke. But if he tried to make a run from the cabin, into the woods, the dogs could track him, stop him, and hold him there. Ted stayed with his team to help rescue her.

A paramedic team was on standby at Ted's house so they could swoop in and care for Marcie on the scene if she needed it.

"Good," Ted said, his eyes never straying from the cabin.

Everything was ready, and everyone was in place.

In the meantime, Officer Wittman needed to place a call to Beverly who was still in Miami. She'd pulled the number from the text messages on Marcie's cell phone.

A female answered, "Hello?"

"Beverly Westwood?"

"Yes," she answered. "Who is this?"

"This is Officer Wittman," she said. "From the Gouldsboro Police Department."

"Has something happened to my house or my dog?" Beverly asked.

"No, both are fine," Officer Wittman said. "I'm calling because your house-sitter, Marcie Hayes, has gone missing."

"Missing?" Beverly squeaked. "Did she take my dog?"

"Yes, missing," Officer Wittman said. "And no, she didn't take Ginger. We have your Ginger and she's fine."

"Then what's the problem?"

Officer Wittman raised an eyebrow. She didn't care for this society woman at all.

Probably too busy sunning herself in Miami to care about anyone else. Unlike those of us in the Pocono Mountains who have to shovel snow.

What's the problem? Does she have no concern for the young woman who is missing?

Her voice came out stern and official. "We need you to

come in, so we can give you your dog and talk to you about Marcie."

"My dog, where is she?"

"She's fine; she's here in Gouldsboro."

Officer Wittman noted that not one iota of concern was shown for Marcie.

The woman wasn't even faking concern. She simply did not care.

"I don't want to fly back to Pennsylvania right now," Beverly said. "Tomorrow I'm having a procedure. I'll call my boyfriend, Zeke; he can fly there and get my dog."

"Good," Officer Wittman said. "You do that. Here's the number to reach us."

"Got it," Beverly said.

The police were hoping that once Beverly hung up, she would call Zeke and that he would call them to schedule a time to pick up the dog.

And that is exactly what Beverly did. She dialed Zeke.

Zeke's cell phone rang.

Beverly.

He answered, "Hello, darling."

"Zeke, I need you to go get that old elf doll!"

Beverly sounded frantic. He smiled as he began to play along. "The elf doll. But, darling, you said you didn't want it in Miami."

"I cannot win the elf contest without it!' Her voice became shriller. "I need that elf! They could kick me off the contest any day! I need you to go get it right away."

"I have a lot of work to finish tonight," he said, as he tested the black ropes now tying Marcie's ankles to the bed, which had replaced the white ones.

She stared up at him, the gag in her mouth preventing her from making noise anywhere but in her throat.

"But perhaps," he placed his hand on Marcie's ankle and began to slide it slowly up her leg, enjoying watching her feeble struggle to move away as those wide eyes watched him. "If Marcie could meet me halfway and bring the doll …"

"No, no, no." Beverly's exasperated voice came over the line. "The girl has gone missing." His hand crept upward, upon the girl in question.

"Missing?" He reached for the knife on his belt and slid the knife underneath the black lace panties he'd placed on Marcie. For tonight's photo session. A new outfit for tonight. And new games. He did like playing with her body. The matching bra dipped low enough that her breasts were almost falling out.

"Yes. The house-sitter you recommended has gone missing," disdain dripped from Beverly's lips, "according to the policewoman who called me. Where did you say you found the girl, again?"

"She house-sat for my cousin," he said, cutting the lace on one side of the panties and reaching for the other side. "He didn't have any problems with her."

"Well, now she's missing. This is your fault for suggesting that I hire her, so you need to fix things," Beverly said.

He cut the other side of the panties, relishing his power over Marcie, as his girlfriend berated him. He pulled the lace panties away and flung them to the floor.

"Yes, dear," he said, which he knew would placate Beverly.

He watched Marcie and slowly began to touch her again. Her skin was smooth and unblemished. He enjoyed touching her, watching her, and tonight we would do more than touch her.

He glanced at the cabinet in the corner, which held the whip inside.

"You'll have to go to the police station to pick Ginger up." Beverly was speaking again and watching Marcie was getting him excited, the thrill of touching her while talking to Beverly turning him on in a new way.

Mentioning the dog again sounded like the afterthought that it was. He knew that Beverly only cared about the little dog when she was in the mood to do so.

"Ginger?" he asked. "What's wrong with Ginger?" Prolonging the conversation so he could keep this thrill going, he wondered how long he could keep Beverly on the line and what it would feel like to take Marcie for the first time, while talking with his girlfriend.

That was something he hadn't contemplated before.

The bossier Beverly was, the more he wanted to control Marcie. He cupped one breast and squeezed.

Helpless, that's what his side girl was. Helpless and beautiful. He needed some photos of her looking just like this before he took her.

"Haven't you been listening? Nothing is wrong with Ginger other than you need to go to the police station and get her back and get that old elf!" Beverly sounded frantic. "I'll never win the contest without it!" Her voice became shriller as she repeated the one thing that had her so riled. "I'm going to get kicked out of the contest!"

Just like mother, he thought.

Her shrill shrieking often happened first thing in the morning, after she'd worked herself up, before he had to get up and get ready for school. Worse than a rooster or an obnoxious alarm, waking him, and though it had been years, he still could not stand hearing women shriek.

His hand had moved up to Marcie's throat and closed around it. Her terrified eyes stared up at him, the gag making her unable to shriek.

There was the fear he hadn't seen in her eyes before. It pleased him. She pleased him.

She wasn't the one who had been shrieking.

Pulling himself together, he removed his hand from her throat and let it drift down to Marcie's soft, left breast as he answered Beverly.

"Darling, I will take care of it," he smiled at Marcie, really speaking to her, as he massaged her breast and then gave it a squeeze. "You know how I take care of you and what you need. I will take care of everything." He smiled.

"Good," Beverly said. "You do that." Then she hung up.

He set his phone on the table beside the bed and pulled the gag down from Marcie's mouth. "You've been a good girl," he said, his tone implying that Beverly had not been.

She licked her lips, her mouth clearly dry, but did not speak. She glanced away from him to the water bottle on the table.

"Water time," he said, reaching for the bottle of water with the straw. "See how I take care of you?"

Her mouth opened and he placed the straw inside of it. Her lips closed around it.

"Drink," he said. "Can't have you getting dehydrated."

She drank, having learned it was best to do as he said, and her thirst compelled her to drink the water.

"I'm going to leave you for a little while," he said. "But first, I want to get some new videos of you. When I come back, I have a new game for us to play."

She drank until he pulled the bottle away. "That's enough for now," he said. "I have a phone call to make."

He replaced the gag over her mouth and patted her cheek. "Good girl," he said. "See how much better it is when you obey me?"

Picking up his phone again, he dialed the police station. "This is Zeke Kingsley," he said. "What is going on out there? Beverly told me you wanted to speak to me."

"Yes, Mr. Kingsley," the person on the other end answered. "We need to speak with you about Marcie Hayes. She's gone missing."

"Missing?" he said. "Oh hell. She's supposed to be house- and dog-sitting for my girlfriend, Beverly. If she's missing, then where's Ginger, Beverly's dog?"

"We have the dog," the officer said. "You can pick her up when you come to the station."

Zeke made an appointment to pick Ginger up, hung up the phone, and turned back to Marcie with a smile.

"We have an hour to video and when I get back, then we will play a new game," he said.

He took the gag out of her mouth again.

She didn't speak and he didn't want her to. She was a fast learner, which meant she was smart. If she went along with what he wanted, smart was fine. If she kept her mouth shut.

Most women never knew when to quit talking.

He didn't have to tell her he was leaving soon because she'd heard everything he'd said.

Once his camera was set up to videotape her, he began posing her again, moving her legs, but always keeping her hands tied, above her head for videos. He liked watching her body move, to get away from his games and was thrilled to finally have a side girl that was so ticklish.

It fascinated him. The things he could get her body to do. The way it reacted.

Tonight was going to be even better as the games got rougher.

When the hour was up, he opened the closet and took a large bull whip out.

Her eyes took the sight of the whip in and widened with the fear he longed to see.

"Now you see, don't you? I am in control. No woman tells me what to do," he said.

"Beverly told you what to do," she said, her defiance suddenly back. "And now you're going to do what she said."

"You're too mouthy," he said. "Do you know what I do with mouthy women?" He laughed. "Just ask my mother."

"I thought you said your mother was dead," she said.

"She is." He gave her a great big smile. "I made sure of it, when I slit her throat with this knife." He patted the knife at his hip.

The one he'd used to cut the panties off her.

Marcie sucked in a breath and held it.

"Good girl," he said. "You're finally starting to learn."

He gave her another injection then, saying, "You might as well sleep now, because it's going to be quite some time before I am back."

Taking the little dog to Miami would be a long trip and he couldn't risk coming back here after visiting the police station. They would be watching him.

His rusty black Mustang sat parked outside.

The spare car that few people knew about was not easy to trace.

He'd paid cash to a private owner for it years ago, minimal paperwork was involved. He hadn't driven it in a few years, so it wasn't listed with his insurance company.

But once he showed up in it, the police would know what he drove.

He watched as Marcie's eyes grew sleepy and then ran his hands all along her body, getting excited again. As he took care of his needs this time, he told himself this would be the last time he would have to wait for her. Tonight, he would fully claim her.

He'd spent too much time taking videos, enjoying her reactions, thinking she wouldn't be discovered missing and that they would have more time.

Since that wasn't the case, he would need to speed their games up when he returned.

Leaving her secured and sleeping, he climbed the basement stairs and headed toward the front door.

He left the whip out, on the bed next to her, so that when she woke, she would see it and her fear could grow.

As he locked the cabin door behind him, he had the growing feeling of being watched.

He narrowed his eyes and, peering as far as he could, surveyed the woods around the cabin. Everything appeared normal. He pocketed the key to the cabin and headed for his car.

Once inside, he started the car and turned the radio up, loud. Heavy metal.

Something Beverly hated. She only listened to pop, unless she had opera tickets, where she would pretend to know something about opera.

He tended to daydream or make lists when she dragged him to the opera, which bored him out of his mind. Still, he would step out to smoke cigars with the men during intermission.

She had tickets for some holiday show in Miami which she would drag him to, which meant packing his tux the next time he flew down.

His mind was on all this as he raced down the dirt road

which led from the cabin. He loved driving fast and there was no one out here to give him a ticket.

Zeke's car came racing down the dirt road, raising dust that the officers and Protectors hidden in the woods saw, long before the car was close.

An officer pulled on the rope which pulled the Stop Sticks across the road, with perfect timing, just before the car reached them.

Zeke's car ran over the Stop Sticks, which punctured the car's tires, and the car stopped.

The officers stepped out from the tree line and headed toward the car to arrest him.

The car door flew open. Zeke lunged out the door and started to run.

K-9 Unit State Police Officer Matt Adams grinned, and Officer Wittman grinned too.

This was what his dog loved to do. Lived to do.

Matt gave the command to his K9, and Lars, a full-blooded Belgian Malinois, sprang into action, racing toward the perp.

Zeke was fit and could run hard.

But Lars was trained for this and chased him down quickly. Leaping up, Lars grabbed ahold of Zeke's arm with a huge bite, making Zeke scream.

Lars, never letting go, pulled the perp down to the ground and kept him there.

Zeke lay on the ground, nearly crying. "Get him off me! Please!"

Matt wasn't calling Lars off until Zeke was cuffed, and Lars would not let loose until Matt gave the command.

The officers approached, proud of the K-9 and enjoying what they had just witnessed.

There was nothing quite like watching a K-9 in action.

The dogs loved to take down their perp; it was a game they were determined to win, and usually did.

Officer Wittman put the cuffs on Zeke Kingsley.

"No woman will ever put me behind bars," he said.

"And yet, that is exactly what I am going to do," she said. "Arrest you and lock you away." The expression on her face showed that she was taking immense pleasure in that.

She tightened the cuffs enough to make him uncomfortable.

"Ow," he complained. "That's too tight."

"Quit your whining," she said.

Once the cuffs were on Zeke, Matt gave the command for Lars to let go.

Which Lars immediately did. Then he stood looking at Matt.

Officer Wittman pushed Zeke into the patrol car and made sure he was secured in the back seat. "You are going away for a long *time,*" she said.

As Zeke was ready to be taken away, in a patrol car, Matt reached into his pocket and pulled out a fluffy bunny.

Lars wagged his tail and was ready to play.

Matt tossed the bunny.

Lars caught it and proceeded to play with it, tossing it up himself and catching it.

These were all games to him, tossing the bunny, chasing, biting, and taking down the perp. He also knew there would be a juicy steak for him tonight, and a lot more praise.

Matt opened the back door of his patrol car and Lars walked over and climbed in. Their job was done for the day.

Zeke rode away on his way to jail, refusing to speak to anyone without his attorney.

~

ONE OF THE MEN, who had entered the basement and found Marcie, untied her, and wrapped her in a sheet, before gathering her up in his arms and carried her up the stairs.

"Going outside now?" she asked. "Need to see the sky and the moon."

"The sun is up," he said. "No moon for a while."

Marcie frowned. "No moon? But it's sleep time."

She'd clearly been drugged, and she was heavy, due to being drugged.

Ted was just outside the cabin waiting for her. "Marcie," he said. "I'm so glad we found you."

"So sleepy," she said.

"Her confusion is from the drugs still in her system," Tanner "Diesel" Taylor said. "He's been injecting her with something. She'll need to be checked out."

"Of course," Ted said. He held out his arms for her, and Diesel placed her in Ted's arms where, even though groggy, she snuggled against him and his arms tightened, more protectingly around her.

He carried her toward the ambulance which was now there.

"Marcie," he said. "The EMT's need to check to make sure you are okay."

""Home, please," she said, barely able to stay awake. "Want to go home," she mumbled.

"He gave her something," Ted told the EMTs. "I don't know what." Then he gently placed Marcie on the gurney.

"No." She opened her eyes and reached for him.

He held her hands instead of lifting her again. "Marcie, I'll take you home as soon as a doctor says that it's okay to take you home," Ted said. "And I'm not going anywhere." He squeezed one of her hands, and let go of the other hand, so the paramedic could get closer. "I'm right here."

"Ginger?" she asked. "And Ace?"

"They're both fine," he said. "I've been taking care of them."

"Zeke Kingsley is crazy," she said.

"He is," Ted agreed.

"He killed his mother. Hates women," she mumbled.

"If he hates women, then why did he take you?"

The paramedics working on her, kept her from going back to sleep, so she watched him through groggy eyes.

"To be a quiet little doll," she said. "Not talk. Dress the doll, undress the doll. Photo time. Pose here. Now pose there. Video time. Play his game."

These details were making Ted's head hurt, or maybe it was the stress of worrying Marcie would be hurt.

He was used to flying jets, not finding and rescuing kidnap victims.

"Lots of pictures," she said. "And videos. He likes to watch me."

"Well, he won't be watching you anymore," Ted said.

"Good," she said. "He is creepy."

Creepy was the word she had used to describe that elf.

"We found a camera in that elf," Ted said. "Or the police found it, I mean. He's been watching you through that elf doll."

"Knew it was creepy," she said. "Ginger knew."

"Yes," he said. "Ginger is a smart little dog, and so are you. I should have listened to you both and paid more attention to that elf."

AT THE HOSPITAL, the doctor checked her over and declared her to be okay, and said that once the drugs wore off and were out of her system, she'd be fine. Though he did suggest some counseling for her ordeal.

Zeke hadn't progressed beyond touching her and playing with her body, but if the police and Ted's Team had been much later, rescuing her, she was sure she would have felt the sting of the whip he'd promised to use on her.

At last, she was home again, in Ted's home.

Ted gathered Marcie into his arms, pulling her close. "You're safe, babe. I've got you."

She nestled into his warmth and his strength, needing it now, wanting to feel safe, to feel loved and cared for. "I was afraid I'd never get away," she said.

"I know, sweet," he said, his hand rubbing her back to warm and comfort her.

The tension in her back started to melt away at his touch.

When it had eased more than a little, he pulled back and gazed into her eyes. "I was worried we wouldn't find you in time," he said.

"You were looking for me?"

"Of course," he said.

Those two simple words soaked into her soul.

Of course, he was looking.

She wasn't alone in the world anymore. She wouldn't disappear off the planet without someone missing her.

That this was a fundamental need had never occurred to her before, but it did now.

She was tired of being a lone wolf, moving about the globe with no attachments. Those days were over. She wanted this now. She wanted Ted Barr.

Her protector. Her lover. The man of her heart.

She was in love with him.

He removed his hands from her waist and raised them up to cup her face. His hands, warm and gentle, pulled her toward him for a kiss, and when their lips met, all the pent-up emotion inside each of them met, each of them giving and loving the other.

It was the kiss of a lifetime; one they would never forget.

"I want you to stay with me," he said, when they came up for air.

This could have meant: Stay with him, instead of staying in that house. Or it could have meant stay here in Pennsylvania, instead of using that airline ticket to fly back to her home base where her storage unit was, and where her mail had piled up. And it did mean those things, but she saw deep within his eyes that he meant something else.

"Stay with me," he repeated.

"Yes," she said. With her whole heart she said yes.

She wanted to stay with him forever, or for as long as he would have her.

But how long would he want her?

As if he'd read that question in her eyes, he said, "Stay with me for the holidays and for as long as you want. I'm asking you to be my girl."

"I think I already am," she smiled.

"You think you are?" he said. "I need you to choose, Marcie. Not to fall into this because it's easy and what you need right now. I'm asking you to make a choice. Do you think you can commit to that? To having someone to come home to? It will mean not living out of a suitcase and not going wherever you want, on a whim, without discussing it with someone who cares about you and wants to be sure you come home safe to him. It'd be a big lifestyle change for you. I just need to know if you're willing to try it."

"I could more than try it," she said. "I could make that change."

"I'm glad," he said.

"I don't need a house," she said. "I never did. I don't need a home. Because you are my home and with you is where I want to be."

A huge smile spread across his face and then he kissed her.

They kissed for a very long time, and he thought, *I could do this for the rest of our lives. If she'll say yes.*

He knew it was too soon, but eventually he planned to ask her to marry him.

For now, they had each other and they were together and that was all that mattered.

AFTER ZEKE WAS ARRESTED and they searched his apartment, they found his boot matched the print taken from the casting. The hair on the towel had been his. The more they found, the more evidence they had to help put him away for a very long time.

From what Marcie had said, they were also looking into his mother's death, to discover if there had been foul play.

And then there were the previous three 'side girls,' which he'd written about in a small journal they found hidden under his mattress, the only two pieces of evidence found in his apartment being his boots and the journal.

The cabin, however, was full of photos and videos, which ranged from sweet and innocent to shocking.

The police knew they had captured a psycho who was a serial killer. They just hadn't found the bodies of the three women he'd written about killing. He'd neglected to note their locations.

Ted would keep up with the investigation because he wanted to know if they got enough evidence to lock Zeke up for life, so that he never got out again.

He didn't want Marcie to be looking over her shoulder for the rest of her life.

"He can lawyer-up all he wants," Officer Schwartz said. "We've got enough just from him kidnapping Marcie, to put him away for a long time. But we would like to find the other three women he called side girls. If his journal is to be believed, all three of those women are dead. Your girl got lucky. She survived."

"And I got lucky that we found her," Ted said. He'd realized something in the short time since he'd known her and during the ordeal. He wanted her in his life, for the rest of their lives. He just needed to tell her and one day he would.

There was one thing he had wanted to ask her, and he was not about to say, 'I told you so,' but that key under the door mat bothered him.

"Marcie, I've waited to bring this up," he hesitated.

"What?" she asked and waited for him to answer.

"The spare key," he said. "I put it on your key ring for you and told you it wasn't safe under the door mat. Why did you take it off?"

She didn't answer him, but instead dug into her purse and pulled out her key ring. "I didn't," she said. "I don't know who put that key there, but I still have this one."

They both suspected who had put it there, but Ted wasn't going to bring his name up again. So, he just nodded, and then gave her a big hug, kissing the top of her head. "I just want to keep you safe," he said.

"And you did," she answered.

"No, I didn't," he said. "I failed."

"You found me," she said. "And that is what matters."

He hugged her closer.

"I do have one thing to ask," she said.

"Name it," he said.

"I don't want to have to go back into that house," she said. "Will you get my things, and the food that I bought, all that stuff?"

"Of course," he said. "You can stay here and play with the pups." He'd noticed how she brightened up when Ginger and Ace were around.

If anyone needed a dog, his Marcie did.

Maybe he could find her one in time for Christmas. They had Ace, but he was very much Teds dog, and she needed a dog of her own.

Officer Wittman had one more call to make.

"What do you mean Zeke has been arrested?" Beverly's voice rose to a shrillness that hadn't been there before.

"Yes, ma'am," Officer Wittman said. "He's been charged with kidnapping Marcie Hayes, your house-sitter."

"Oh, that's ridiculous," Beverly said. "He's been with me. He can't have done that. He wouldn't."

"Actually," Officer Wittman said, "He would, and he did. He's been with Marcie, in his cabin in the woods, and we caught him there."

"What?" Beverly went speechless, likely from the shock.

Officer Wittman gave her a pause for that to sink in and then said gently, "So, we'll need you to come get Ginger, as he won't be able to do that for you."

"What?" Beverly's voice was back to normal. "No. I'm not

coming up there for any reason. Keep my name out of this, I don't want to be related to him in any way."

"You already are."

"Well, you just keep my name quiet then, no newspapers or television," Beverly retorted. "I'll be contacting my lawyer."

"And Ginger?" Officer Wittman reminded her.

"Keep her," Beverly said. "I don't want her. Or that damn elf, which I never wanted in the first place. That was all his idea. I can't believe this is happening."

"So, you don't want your dog?" Officer Wittman asked again, to be sure.

"No." Beverly said. "I do not want anything to remind me of Zeke Kingsley. The dog, the elf, the house. I am washing my hands of anything and everything that would remind me of him. I'll put the house on the market as soon as I call my lawyer. If you need anything else from me, you'll have to go through him."

"All right then," Officer Wittman said. "I'm sure we can find a good home for Ginger."

"Whatever," Beverly said.

She hung up.

Officer Wittman sat looking at her phone for a moment and then shook her head.

She decided to head over to Ted's house to give him the latest update in person. If she were a betting person, she'd bet money that Ted or Marcie would be happy to take the dog.

As she pulled up in front of Ted's house, she saw Ted and Marcie out front with the dogs, either heading out for a walk or coming back from one.

It was hard to tell as they had stopped on the side of the road in front of his house and were kissing.

Officer Wittman grinned. Sometimes she got to see a happy ending, which was a big plus in her line of work. She had a feeling their happy ending was going to get a whole lot happier.

They broke away and watched her park her patrol car in his driveway.

She got out and headed over to them. "Good morning," she said.

"Good morning," they both greeted her.

"I spoke to Beverly just a little bit ago," she said.

"Oh lord," Marcie said. "What now? I suppose she's headed here to get her dog."

"Actually, no, she isn't," Officer Wittman said.

Ginger was wanting attention, so Marcie scratched her ear.

Ted said, "Why not?"

"Oh, I can guess," Marcie said. "She's expecting me to deliver Ginger to her. That's just the kind of thing she would expect."

"No, not at all. She doesn't want her name mentioned in the papers or to be anywhere near the crime scene, and the dog isn't worth the bad publicity. She's not coming to get her."

"Ever?" Marcie appeared stunned.

"Correct," Officer Wittman said. "So, if you want Ginger, she's yours."

"Really?" Marcie's eyes widened and joy spread across her face. "Of course, I want her."

She turned toward Ted. "Oh, Ted, isn't that wonderful news? I get to keep Ginger!"

"That is fantastic news," he said.

As Officer Wittman drove away, she thought, *a happy ending for all of them. Now that makes my day.*

Her face broke into a smile that would not quit.

THE END

AFTERWORD

If you enjoyed reading my newest story, *To Catch an Elf,* I hope you will take the time to leave a review anywhere.

Even a short one line review is more helpful than you know. They are essential to a books success.

I read every single one, and I love to hear what you think of my books.

ACKNOWLEDGMENTS

It takes a team to put good books out into the world and I appreciate the team who helped me to put To Catch an Elf out there for you all to read.

My cover artist, Sheri L. Mcgathy created this amazing cover, which captures the creepy elf so well. Thank you for all the wonderful covers you create for my books. I especially like this one.

This story would not have been completed nearly as well without the help of former LEO Charlene Leber Lancaster as I had reached a point where I was stumped. It turns out that catching a serial killer on paper is hard. At least it was for me. He'd still be running loose if not for Charlene being my beta reader.

Thank you to the Bartlett Citizens Police Academy for the ten weeks of training, which gave me a base of knowledge to write from. I loved watching you guys train your K-9 companions. They are the most amazing dogs. So I had to write one into the story. Lars in this story, is in honor of the real life Lars from the Bartlett, TN Police force.

Proficient proofreading was done by Melissa Ammons, who also works as my virtual assistant and does more for me than I could possibly list here.

Thank you to my husband, Mike, who is so much more than the bus driver of our 43 foot rig. I have needed his help with so many things since my stroke. Forty two years together and we are still having adventures, which I am thankful for.

Thank you to everyone who has come to my twelve days of creepy elf party for years. You've waited on this book to be done for a very long time. In the meantime, we've had lots of fun at those parties. I'm excited to be celebrating this books release this year during the party and hope you all can come. (It's in my Facebook group.)

Thank you to all my new readers who have taken a chance on reading this book. I hope it keeps you turning the pages, and that you enjoy the story.

Thank you to all my steadfast readers who have read so many of my books. Yes, this one took a long time to finish. I hope you feel it was worth the wait. I love being able to share my stories with you.

To my reviewers, who take the time to read and to review my books, I appreciate you! Reviews are essential to a book's success and I love hearing what you think of my stories.

And most of all, thank you God, for helping me to survive that stroke, this past June, and for always keeping me safe while I walked around unaware of the blood clot in my brain. For regaining the ability to read a line of text and the ability to write my stories and to finally finish this one. And for surrounding me with so many people who care for me and prayed daily and continue to pray for my healing.

Every day we are alive is a beautiful day, and I am thankful every single day for that.

ABOUT THE AUTHOR

Author Debra Parmley believes "Every day we are alive is a beautiful day," and she likes to give her readers and her story people a story that ends happily.

An Air Force veteran's wife, Debra writes suspense, military romantic suspense, contemporary romance, historical romance, urban fantasy romance, fairy tale romance, holiday romance, poetry, and memoir.

Debra married her high school sweetheart, whom she asked out after a five-dollar bet. After living in five states with her husband and their two sons, and then living 23 years just outside Memphis, TN, she and her husband sold everything in 2020 and now live and travel the U.S. in their 43-foot motorhome.

Debra is an adventurous writer who has worked as an independent travel agent and set foot in more than 13 countries. She has walked the plank of a pirate ship off the coast of Grand Cayman, and has gone swimming with dolphins in Moorea, French Polynesia. She once escorted a bus full of people through Scotland.

She climbs lighthouses because she is afraid of heights.

You can see read about her travels on her Beautiful Day Traveler blog. https://beautifuldaytraveler.wordpress.com/

As Debra Bishop, she writes fairy tales for all ages, fantasy, and children's books.

Visit www.debraparmley.com

MILITARY ROMANTIC SUSPENSE:

Green Brotherhood SEAL Team XII series:

Finding Bryce, book one - eBook, paperback

Real Movie Hero, book two - eBook, paperback

Saving the Bellydancer, book three - eBook, paperback

Green Brotherhood Trilogy #1 - eBook boxset

Brotherhood Protectors series:

Montana Marine - book one - eBook, paperback

Defensive Instructor - book two -eBook, paperback

Marine Protector - book three- eBook, paperback

Marine Protectors - box set - eBook.

Blind Trust - book four - eBook, paperback

A Triple C Ranch Christmas Wedding - book five - eBook, paperback

Montana Delta Rescue - book six - eBook, paperback

Montana SEAL Protector - book seven - eBook, paperback

Montana Rodeo Protector - book eight - eBook, paperback – Dec. 2023 or 2024

Montana White Horse Wedding – book nine eBook, paperback - 2024

~

Bobbins Sisters Trilogy:

Check Out – book one, eBook, paperback, audiobook.

Check In – book two, eBook, paperback.

Check Mate – book three - 2024.

~

Single Title:

Aboard the Wishing Star - eBook, paperback, audiobook

~

SUSPENSE -THRILLER – with Romance:

To Catch an Elf – eBook, paperback, Large Print Hardcover

~

URBAN FANTASY ROMANCE:

Vague Directions – Dec. 2023

~

WESTERN HISTORICAL ROMANCE:

Gone to Texas: A Desperate Journey - (original sweeter version) -
Large Print Hardcover, eBook, paperback.

Dangerous Ties - eBook, paperback, audiobook

Deadly Adversaries - eBook, paperback

Desperate, Dangerous, Deadly: A Western Collection – eBook box set

Isabella, Bride of Ohio: American Mail Order Bride – (original sweeter version) - Large Print Hardcover, eBook, paperback

Penny From Deadwood - coming 2024

1920's ROMANCE:

Butterflies Fly Free series:

Trapping the Butterfly – book one, eBook, paperback, audiobook, Large Print Hardcover

Dancing Butterfly – book two, eBook, paperback

Exotic Butterfly – book three, 2024

HOLIDAY ROMANCE:

Jenna's Christmas Wish – eBook, paperback

The Twelve Stitches of Christmas – (short story – fairy tale) – eBook

DYSTOPIAN ROMANCE:

The Hunger Roads Trilogy:

Another Change of Scenery – 2024

Down a Back Road – 2024

Into the Convergence Zone – 2024

NONFICTION:

Anywhere But Here: Our First Year Full Time RV Living on the Road – 2024

POETRY:

Anthology: Twilight Dips – eBook, print

Out of Print:

Protecting Pippa

Split Screen Scream

Protecting Zarifah

Vague Directions – short story

A Desperate Journey

Isabella, Bride of Ohio

Tales of Deadwood - anthology

We Know the Truth, Do You? Area 51 – anthology (going to the moon/time capsule)

Wounded Heroes - anthology

Hansel & Gretel: Down the Rabbit Hole – anthology

More Monsters from Memphis – anthology

WRITING AS DEBRA BISHOP:

Fairytales for all ages:

The Sweetest Day - Hansel and Gretel fairytale - eBook, paperback

Fantasy:

The Rolling House – time travel serial fiction – ongoing story.

Gatalop – 2024

Bellserie – 2024

Children's: coming in 2024.